In Memory
of Michael

Other titles in
the Hammond Cousins Series
by Wanda Yoder

Markie and the Hammond Cousins

Markie is part of the Hammond clan, but he's mentally handicapped. The cousins are sure they'll be embarrassed. Instead, they learn to love one of God's special children.

Ricky and the Hammond Cousins

The Hammond cousins are first bewildered, then exasperated, and finally compassionate as they learn to relate to a boy with a hyperactive disorder.

In Memory of Michael

by Wanda Yoder

Christian Light Publications, Inc.
Harrisonburg, Virginia 22801-1212

Christian Light Publications, Inc. Harrisonburg, Virginia 22801
© 1998 by Christian Light Publications, Inc.
All rights reserved. Published 1998
Printed in the United States of America

07 06 05 04 03 02 01 00 99 98   5 4 3 2 1

Cover by Michelle Beidler

ISBN: 0-87813-577-4

Dedication

Written in memory of Jonathan Lee Yoder,
stillborn May 5, 1989,
And dedicated to our seven living children
for whom many of the feelings and inci-
dents included in this book are very real.

Wanda Yoder

Contents

Chapter 1

Getting Ready

There. As nearly as she could tell, there was not a drip on the entire baby crib. Marilyn Hammond sat back and surveyed the crib with satisfaction, her paintbrush held over the can of white paint. Excitement surged through her. Wouldn't it be wonderful to have a tiny baby lying there!

This crib had held her and her three younger sisters when they were babies. But a new baby was coming! Marilyn had worked a long time getting the crib ready. She had not minded the paint stripper's stinging fumes as she scraped off layers of pink, yellow, and dusty blue paint. Now the crib was a pure white, the proper color for a baby crib, according to Marilyn and her sisters.

She looked up when the garage service door opened. In came six-year-old Rita with a reddish brown chicken tucked under her arm.

"Shut the door, Rita," Marilyn said. "It's rainy out, and I want the paint to dry. I'm glad Dad let me start a fire in this old trash burner, or it would be too cold in here."

Rita walked all around the crib, making sure her dress did not touch the wet paint. Slowly a smile brightened her often sober little face. "I can hardly believe it," she breathed. "It's so beautiful. Now I *know* there is going to be a baby!"

Marilyn laughed gaily. "Of course, there is going to be a baby. Mother told you so. Isn't it exciting?"

Rita nodded and stood silently, stroking the feathers of the hen.

"Why don't you put Iona back into the chicken house?" Marilyn asked.

"She misses me on Kindergarten Days," the little girl explained. "So I play with her all I can."

"I imagine it's rather you missing her," Marilyn observed. Everyone in the family knew Rita's pet helped make her happy. After their dog Ronald had gotten run over last summer,

Rita quietly adopted Iona from their flock of mixed breed chickens. The little Rhode Island Red thrived on her attention.

As Marilyn looked up, the door burst open, and eight-year-old Suzanne bounced into the room, brushing against the crib. The door slammed shut behind her.

"Are you finished?" she asked.

"Well, I was until you smudged the railing," Marilyn said, picking up the brush and smoothing the paint.

"Oops. Sorry. Didn't mean to do that. Say, that looks nice except this little place on the end. The paint kind of sags or something."

Marilyn patiently repaired the sag for her critical little sister. "You'd better check your dress. Mother won't like if you've gotten paint on it. Why didn't you change into an everyday dress?"

Suzanne shrugged. "It's dirty anyway. I sat down in a mud puddle at school. I don't see why it has to rain all the time in April. It's warm enough during the day, if it just wouldn't rain."

"April showers bring May flowers. That's why," Rita said solemnly. "Sister Ruth said so."

"And May babies," Marilyn reminded them with a teasing smile.

3

Again the door opened. The third sister entered. Like little Rita, she took her time inspecting the crib. "It's lovely," she praised sincerely. "You've even gotten rid of Rita's tooth marks on the top rail. How did you do that? They were deep."

Marilyn laughed. "It took a lot of sanding, I can tell you. But it was worth it."

Twila's dark eyes became dreamy. "There's only one thing that would improve it now," she said. "And that's some little animals or flowers or butterflies painted on the ends for the baby to look at."

"Teddy bears," Rita said. "Babies like teddy bears."

"Balloons," Suzanne said emphatically. "The Webers bought a brand-new crib for their baby, and it had balloons painted on the ends, all different colors. And they had balloons on the wallpaper and on the curtains . . ."

"Wait a minute!" Marilyn said. "If it's up to me, there won't be anything painted on this crib. If I tried, I'd make a mess of it. Twila, if Mother helps you, I suppose you could try. You can paint on paper. Painting pictures on a crib shouldn't be any harder."

"If it doesn't turn out, you can always paint

over it," Suzanne said, grinning mischievously at her ten-year-old sister. "It probably won't look nice anyway."

"Don't be so negative," Marilyn said. "With Mother's help, it could look great."

Mother opened the door. "I hate to disturb your industry," she smiled. "But Dad's going to be home any minute, and I hope we can sit down to the supper table when he comes."

Rita trudged off to return Iona to the chicken house. The two middle sisters skipped into the house chattering happily about the crib and the coming baby. Marilyn carefully cleaned the rim on the top of the paint can and tapped the lid tightly shut. Dad was very fussy about things like that. She put the brush in a can of paint cleaner.

Just then there was a crunching of tires on the gravel outside and the sound of an engine. The garage door whined slowly open. Dad was home. He drove his work truck inside, the motor noise echoing loudly in the garage.

Marilyn waited. She cared more about Dad's opinion than anyone else's. He was a finish carpenter, and careful work was important to him.

He looked over the crib closely. "You did a fine job," he said sincerely. "A very fine job, especially for a thirteen-year-old. I'm pleased with your work." His eyes twinkled. "Maybe this summer we should take you to the job with us."

"Not a chance," Marilyn returned. "Not with a baby in the house!"

They went into the house laughing.

"Well, how was your day?" Mother asked as she passed the potatoes after prayer. Nearly every evening she asked the same question, and usually Dad answered with interesting stories of his day at work.

"We started on the drywall in the Rucker house today," Dad said. "The only bad thing is the twenty-foot-high ceiling in the living room."

Mother frowned. "I hope you let the young fellows do the high jobs."

"Oh, I do my part," Dad said casually. "Just be glad I'm not a window washer on skyscrapers like those we saw in Chicago last summer!"

"Well, that would be worse," Mother agreed.

"Our neighbor, Bob Graham, was at the job site today working on the plumbing. I chatted with him quite a while during lunch break."

Marilyn looked up with interest. The summer before, she had mowed lawn several times for the Grahams when Mr. Graham was too busy. "Did he have anything special to say? Does

6

he want me to mow their lawn this summer?"

"As a matter of fact, he was wondering if you could do even more than that," Dad said. "His wife needs some help. She is a diabetic–has been ever since she was a teenager. She had some sores on one leg that wouldn't heal, and three weeks ago the leg had to be amputated."

"Amputated? What does that mean?" Suzanne interrupted.

"Cut off. Completely cut off. She's been staying with her mother over at Deer Creek, but Mr. Graham would like to bring her home. He wants to take care of her himself as much as possible."

"I've never seen Mrs. Graham," Mother said. "Did you ever see her when you mowed lawn, Marilyn?"

"Never. She was always gone somewhere. And I only saw Mr. Graham once, when he showed me how to run the lawnmower. How old are they, Dad?"

"Not so much older than we are. He told me today he is 45, and his wife a few years younger. I've always liked Bob Graham. We've worked on a number of the same houses. He is one of the few worldly men I've never heard swear or use questionable language. Yet once when I asked him whether he was a Christian, he said he guessed he was, that he wasn't a heathen anyway. But he wouldn't comment any further. Perhaps by helping them we can leave a Christian witness."

"What does he want Marilyn to do?" Mother wondered. "She's pretty young to be doing much other than lawn work and that sort of thing. Oh, I know she knows quite a bit about housework, but I'm not sure she's ready for a lot of that kind of responsibility."

After Dad finished eating his apple crisp, he went on, "Mr. Graham just wondered if Marilyn could check in on his wife for an hour or so after school to see that she's comfortable, run errands, and start supper. He would fix lunch at home, but the afternoons could seem long for his wife. Or a problem could come up before he came home in the evening. Would you mind that, Marilyn, until school is out?"

"It would be kind of scary," Marilyn said honestly. Her stomach felt funny at the thought of going into a home so different from her own.

"Imagine having your leg cut off," Suzanne marveled. "It gives me the creeps to think about it."

8

"It doesn't take much to give you the creeps," Dad said dryly. "But it is sad, that's for certain. I think Mrs. Graham is a naturalist and used to spend most of her time outside studying plants. Mr. Graham said she's bitter, because now she's pretty much confined to the house. Her career is wrecked."

"What about when the baby comes?" Twila asked. "Does that mean *I* get to take care of the baby instead of Marilyn?" Her dark eyes sparkled with enthusiasm.

"Well, some of these things can be discussed further," Dad smiled. "Thanks for the supper, Mother. If you don't mind, I have some re-arranging to do on the truck. Maybe you should rest until I come back in. These girls look anxious to do the dishes."

Marilyn began washing the dishes, and Rita began to dry. Twila swept the floor under the dining room table, and Suzanne spread her homework out on the tiny kitchen table so Marilyn could help her if necessary.

"I have to do this community map over again," she stormed. "Sister Ruth said it wasn't neat enough."

"Well, I wondered last evening whether it would pass," Marilyn said. "Why don't you try

9

making each letter in your labels just perfect, and each color nice and even."

"I think this is an interesting project," Twila said, bending over her younger sister's shoulder. Sister Ruth had drawn a map of the community, and her students were to label the little houses representing all the church family homes. Then they were to color the map neatly and add other things of interest.

"Well, you would. You like being p'tickler. But it's not my cup of tea."

Marilyn turned so her colorful little sister wouldn't see her amusement.

"Mother doesn't like for us to fuss about our schoolwork. She says schoolwork is our work for now, and we'd better do the best we can," Twila said seriously.

"I know," Suzanne admitted with a sigh as her little brown head bent industriously over her work again. Marilyn wondered if it would look neater this time.

Rita stood quietly on her stool and dried the dishes. "And what *are* we going to name the baby?" she asked suddenly.

"Mother and Dad named all of us," Marilyn reminded her. "I suppose they won't ask us. But what would you choose to name it, if it's a girl?"

"But I hope it's a boy," Rita said wistfully.

"So do I. We all do, I suppose," Marilyn said.

Just then Mother walked through. "I have four sweet girls," she said. "I won't mind a fifth, if that's what God gives us. What were you saying about names, Rita?"

"What are we going to name the baby?" the little girl persisted, a worried pucker between her eyes.

"Dad and I will decide," Mother said. "But we'll take suggestions if you have some."

"I like *M* names," Marilyn said. "I'm glad my name starts with an *M*. For a boy it could be Marvin, Milton, Morris, Matthew, Micah . . ."

Suzanne suddenly lifted her head from her schoolwork. "Or Mahershalalhashbaz. That starts with *M*. It's a Bible name. The longest name in the Bible. Sister Ruth said so."

"It won't work," Rita said solemnly.

"I guess it won't!" Mother agreed, laughing.

"I mean it won't work," Rita repeated. "There's not enough room at the top of the paper. Teacher always puts a line for our names. Mahershbaz won't fit."

Twila giggled. "Oh, Rita, you're funny, but you're right. A name like that would be a nuisance. Mother, will the baby have a Bible name?"

"Perhaps," Mother said. "But Bible names have been a bit over-used in this community. It can get confusing. We'll see. Dad and I feel we make our names honorable and appreciated by how we live, rather than our names forming our character. But we do want our children to have good, practical names."

"Myrtle. That's an *M* name," Suzanne's green eyes were dancing. "If we have a girl, would you like to name her Myrtle? Myrtle Miller is a nice woman."

Myrtle was an honorable woman, but somehow Marilyn didn't like the name, not when it rhymed with *turtle*. "There are other nice names," she said. "I guess we can all give Mother our ideas, but I hope she and Dad come up with two better than Mahershalalhashbaz and Myrtle!"

"It sounds like we're getting a bit silly," Mother said. "Come out to the greenhouse with me for a little while. We can get the rest of the tomato plants transplanted, and then it will be bedtime. I think the rain has stopped. It smells nice and spring-like outside."

Mother planted vegetable and flower plants for several of the women of the church along with flats for their own big garden. The girls enjoyed helping. It was a special rite of spring-time.

But as they all squished across the yard, Marilyn knew her smallest sister was thinking of tiny babies rather than tiny tomato plants. "Elmer, Isaac, Fred, Sam, Benny . . ." Marilyn heard Rita whispering.

Chapter 2

Mrs. Graham's Need

The way home from school had never seemed so short to Marilyn as it did this day in mid-April.

"Dad said the key is under the welcome sign hanging on the left side of the door. You are just to let yourself in, because Mrs. Graham cannot get up very easily," Mother instructed Marilyn as they drove in the Grahams' lane.

"How will she know it's me?" Marilyn asked nervously. "Maybe she'll think I'm a burglar!"

"It would probably be wise to call out who you are in case she can't see you when you come in. And be cheerful, Marilyn. I think she needs your smile more than your work. Do you want me to come in with you? I could this first time."

Marilyn shook her head. It was not easy for

Mother to get in and out of the car. "No, I'll be all right, I guess. Is Dad going to pick me up at five?"

"Yes, and if you have any problems before then, just call home."

"You look scared," Suzanne said bluntly. "She can't hurt you. She has her leg cut off, so she can't even walk."

"I think Marilyn has flutterbys in her tummy," Rita said with solemn six-year-old wisdom.

"Butterflies," Marilyn corrected, giving her little sister a quick hug. "But you're right," she whispered. Rita's funny way of saying things cheered her up a bit. She got out of the car and hesitantly walked up the brick-paved path.

Why should I be frightened of helping a neighbor? she wondered. Surely Mrs. Graham wouldn't be that different from other women she knew. Or would she? Marilyn would soon find out.

She found the key, opened the door, and entered the hallway. "It's Marilyn Hammond," she called out in a quavering voice that didn't sound at all like her own.

"Come into the living room," a voice ordered.

Mrs. Graham was a big, rawboned woman,

who filled up most of her large recliner. She had dark, gray-streaked hair cut close to her head, almost like a man's. She was wearing a bright purple housecoat. An afghan draped across her lap and down to the floor.

"Well, let's get it over with," Mrs. Graham said roughly. She drew back the afghan and exposed her stump. Her leg had been cut off just below the knee. Only a piece of gauze covered the still unhealed end.

Marilyn stepped back, a wave of dizziness sweeping over her.

"Ugly, isn't it?" Mrs. Graham said. "And that's the end of my career. It's the end of everything, really." Her voice was hard.

"Oh, no, it isn't," Marilyn disagreed instinctively. "It can't be. You can get an artificial leg after awhile, can't you? And then you can do things again."

"Diabetics don't heal as easily as other people do," Mrs. Graham said. "I'm probably stuck here for the rest of my life. Bright prospect!" she added bitterly.

Marilyn was frightened. What could she do for this unhappy woman?

She tried to sound cheerful. "What can I do to help you right now?"

Mrs. Graham's voice softened. "I'm afraid I've scared you. You're so young. You probably haven't seen much suffering and ugliness. I'll try to keep my troubles to myself. Bob left a list of things on the kitchen counter he'd like you to do. He did a lot of the work around here anyway, because I've been away so much. But now he can't keep up with everything."

Marilyn read the list and began the simple tasks. First she sorted the trash into the recycling bins. Then she emptied the dishwasher and tidied the kitchen. After that, she washed two potatoes, wrapped them for the microwave, and made a lettuce salad. Meat was already cooking in a tiny Crock-Pot.

This isn't too bad, Marilyn thought. But she was relieved when she heard Dad drive in the lane. "Good-bye, Mrs. Graham. My father's here now," she said.

"You are an efficient miss, I can tell," Mrs. Graham commented. "Bob will be pleased. He's been so worried. As your father suggested, we'll pay you at the end of the week."

Mrs. Graham looked more cheerful now. The hard look that sometimes froze onto the unhappy woman's face made Marilyn uncomfortable.

"Well, how did it go?" Dad asked as they started home. "Or maybe you can tell us at the supper table. We'll all want to know." They drove the half mile west and then the half mile north that separated the Hammonds from the Grahams.

Mother and the girls certainly did want to know. The chatter at the supper table was all about Mrs. Graham. When Marilyn described Mrs. Graham's leg, Rita's eyes got big. "I sure wouldn't want one of my legs pampupated," she declared. "I need them both."

"It's too bad," Mother agreed. "But even worse is Mrs. Graham's struggle accepting what's happened. It wouldn't be easy. We must pray for her."

The more they discussed it, the more Marilyn felt cheering up Mrs. Graham was more than she could do. "I want to be a Christian witness, but I'll never know what to say," she said desperately.

Dad nodded. "That's often true for people who have been Christians many years. Don't be overly concerned about what to say. Your first responsibility is tending to Mrs. Graham's physical comforts and doing the other work they ask. You can give a cup of cold water in Jesus' name.

I'm sure that is all the Lord requires of you for now."

"It would be nice if Mrs. Graham would become a Christian," Twila said. "Christians don't fuss so much when they have troubles."

"That's true," Mother agreed. "At least that's the way we ought to be. But we've been so blessed. Sometimes I think we've had so little trouble, we don't really know how we would respond."

"Well, you wouldn't act like Mrs. Graham," Suzanne said firmly.

"I was thinking if you girls get these dishes done, it would be a fine evening to go over to Grandma Hammonds," Dad said when the meal was over.

Mother nodded, and the girls bounced up from the table like four Ping-Pong balls. "Yes, let's!" they chorused.

The dishes were done in a remarkably short time.

It was only three miles to Grandma Hammond's place. Dad parked in front of the trailer where Grandma now lived. Uncle Jerry, Aunt Julia, and Ricky lived in the big house where Grandma used to live. The old willow tree sheltered the trailer on the west side, and some newly planted evergreens would form a windbreak to the north. Already, inside and out, the place seemed to fit Grandma Hammond.

She met them at the door. "Why, Alex and Mary Ann, I'm very glad to see you. And girls, come right on in." She gave the girls each a quick hug. She knew how to make children feel extra special.

The three younger girls ran to the back bedroom where Grandma had a doll bed full of hand-made rag dolls and a small suitcase full of doll clothes. They were soon busy playing house. Ten-year-old Twila did not often play with dolls at home because she'd rather read, but she could never resist playing with Grandma's dolls.

Marilyn checked Grandma's violets to see if any new ones were blooming. Grandma had given her violets away when she moved into the trailer, but somehow she was already collecting a new assortment. Grandma Hammond and violets just went together.

Before long there was a knock at the door. It was eight-year-old Ricky. "Grandma, Mama and Daddy said we'll come over and visit a bit, if you don't mind. We won't be a bit of trouble. I promise!" He hopped on one foot and then another, waiting for Grandma's reply.

Grandma looked at Mother and Dad and chuckled. "Tell them to come on over, Ricky. The more the merrier."

With a whoop and a holler, he dashed back home. Soon Uncle Jerry and Aunt Julia came over. Mother knew it got noisy and rowdy when Ricky played with the younger girls, so she wisely sent them outside.

Suzanne and Ricky were the same age and got along remarkably well. She was a tolerant child and put up with Ricky's endless chatter and thoughtless actions. But it was often her blunt advice that kept him out of trouble at school or when the children played together.

Marilyn liked to listen to the grown-ups talk. She marveled at how well Aunt Julia fit into the Hammond family. Aunt Julia had easily made the transition from schoolteacher to wife and mother. Uncle Jerry seemed happier than Marilyn ever remembered seeing him. The sad look no longer lingered in his eyes.

Ricky still needed a lot of attention to keep him under control. But in spite of his learning and behavior problems, he was a happy boy.

"Well, those little ones are probably working up an appetite for cookies," Grandma said after awhile. "Marilyn, would you like to mix up some Kool-Aid while I get out the cookies?"

Marilyn had the drink ready and was at the door calling the younger ones, when another car drove in.

Ricky raced up to the car and skidded to a stop. When the car door opened, Sue stepped out. "You're all by yourself?" Ricky asked in a shocked voice. "You can't drive. Where's Aunt Faith and Uncle Nathan?"

Sue laughed. "They're at home. I can drive. I'm a big girl now, Ricky. I've had my driver's license for quite awhile."

"It ain't safe," he said bluntly. "Driving's for older people."

"Well, I'm old enough. I'm sixteen. May I come in?"

"Oh, sure. The more the merrier. That's what Grandma says. But I still say it ain't safe." Ricky ran into the house to tell his folks about Sue's driving.

"Hi, Marilyn," Sue smiled. "Would you like me to help you serve that drink? Grandma, Mother sent me over to return this apron pattern. She said you were hoping to use it yet this week."

"Thank you," Grandma said. "So now you

are allowed to drive by yourself? That's a stepping-stone, Sue."

Marilyn could not imagine herself driving a car. Why, only last year she accidentally drove the riding lawn mower into a flower bed when one of the girls had distracted her. Dad had told her she would have to learn to be more careful before she could drive a car. "You have to watch where you're going," Dad had said.

Sometimes Marilyn felt as if Sue were suddenly much older than she. They had always played together as little girls, but now Sue was almost a woman, and Marilyn was somewhere in between. But Sue was always a dear, and Marilyn valued her friendship. "What have you been doing with yourself lately?" Sue asked as they sat on the bed in Grandma's back bedroom eating cookies and drinking Kool-Aid.

Marilyn told her about working for Mrs. Graham. "It kind of scares me," Marilyn finished.

Sue smiled reassuringly. "Well, your sweet, friendly ways will be as good a way as any to show her God's love. I'm sure you'll do just fine, Marilyn."

Marilyn felt comforted. She almost looked forward to seeing Mrs. Graham again the next day.

When they were leaving for home, Ricky trailed them to their cars. As Sue slid behind the steering wheel, he warned, "Now you be careful, Sue. You really ain't old enough for driving." She laughed and waved.

On the way home, Marilyn felt content as she and her family traveled through the balmy night. At a swampy area along the road, Dad stopped for a few moments so they could listen to the spring peepers. The air smelled of earth and green things growing.

"We've had a nice time," Rita said sleepily from her corner in the car. "But when the baby comes, it'll be perfecter."

They all chuckled quietly in agreement. No one bothered to correct her grammar.

Chapter 3

Michael's Birth

Marilyn closed her math book and sighed with relief. It was not that she disliked math so much, but tonight so many other thoughts kept getting mixed up with her algebra.

Mother looked up from where she was putting the final crochet stitches in the baby's afghan. "All done?" she asked.

"Yes, finally. Mother, I keep thinking about Mrs. Graham. Sometimes I think she is absolutely the unhappiest person there could ever be. And I'm supposed to cheer her up! Mother, I think it's impossible!"

"Perhaps," Mother agreed. "She has to want to be cheered up first. And she needs the Lord. But Bob told Dad Mrs. Graham seems to appreciate having you come. And Bob certainly does.

He has a lot of confidence in your ability to help his wife."

"Well, helping her depresses me. I think it must be contagious!"

"Is it that bad?" Mother sympathized. "Is it getting you down spiritually?"

"Not really," Marilyn said slowly. "Actually, I think I've prayed more since going to help Mrs. Graham than I ever did before. When she's in her grouchy moods, I pray I won't aggravate her worse. But I've gone there almost every day for two and a half weeks now, and I don't believe she's one bit happier. Her leg doesn't seem any better either."

"Well, just do the best you can. After the baby is here, perhaps I can go over sometimes too. We want to be Christian neighbors. This chance is too good to miss."

Just then Twila came in. "The crib is dry at last," she bubbled. "Let's bring it in. I want to see how it looks in the bedroom."

They all gathered in the garage. After Marilyn had painted the crib, Twila had spent many happy evenings carefully painting butterflies, flowers, and birds on it. Though the colors weren't accurate, the details were exact and neat.

Dad helped them fold the crib and carry it into the house to a little room next to Mother and Dad's bedroom. A storage room before, now it was to be the baby's room.

The girls put the new mattress inside the crib, covered it with a sheet, and folded the blankets Mother had washed. The baby's new afghan lay on top.

"It looks absolutely gorgeous," Rita whispered.

"You are a great artist," Suzanne told Twila. "I expected you to make a mess; instead, our baby will have the prettiest crib in the country. Even prettier than the Webers'. And we're going to have a prettier baby too!"

"Whoa, there," Dad said. "That's no way to talk. We'll just be glad if the baby is healthy. The crib does look very nice though, Twila."

"Well, everything's ready now. I wish we didn't have to wait a couple weeks yet for the baby," Suzanne said.

Mother shooed them from the baby room. "The best thing for you girls now is your beds, instead of dreaming over a baby crib."

"In other words, dream in our own beds," Marilyn laughed.

Soon the house was quiet.

"Marilyn, Marilyn," Dad's voice kept calling. Marilyn's sleepy eyes blinked and turned toward her alarm clock. Its lighted dial showed 1:30 a.m. *Why is Dad trying to wake me at this time of the night?* she wondered groggily.

"Marilyn!" Dad said softly. "I'm taking Mother to the hospital now. I just wanted you to know." There was an urgency in his voice.

Questions bounced to the surface of her mind and a thrill of excitement. "Oh, Dad! I hope everything goes all right," she whispered back.

So the baby is a bit early. The younger girls will be so excited in the morning, Marilyn thought. She was tempted to go to the bed across their room and wake Twila. She would be so thrilled. But then neither of them would be able to sleep. Marilyn turned over and tried to control the waves of excitement that kept coursing through her. At last she fell asleep.

When her alarm rang at 6:45, Marilyn pulled on her housecoat and walked through the silent house. Usually Dad and Mother were up, but this morning it was obvious they were gone. She went to the kitchen for a drink. While her glass was filling with water, a car drove in the lane. It was Dad. He did not park in the garage. Marilyn ran to meet him at the door.

Dad came in, carefully closed the door, and turned toward Marilyn. "Well, you have a little brother," he said slowly.

A cold ribbon of fear raced through Marilyn. *What's wrong? Why doesn't Dad look happy?*

Before she could ask, Dad said, "Go get the other girls up. I may as well explain everything at once."

Marilyn's stomach felt weak, but she did as she was told. In a few moments, the four stood expectantly in their robes at the dining room doorway.

"You have a little brother," Dad repeated.

"Goody! Goody!" Suzanne squealed. "It's about time! What did you name him, Dad?"

"Michael Alex." Dad reached for a chair and sat down heavily. "But, girls, we may not be able to keep him."

The sisters stood in stunned silence as Dad quietly explained. "You see, there's something wrong with Michael's heart. As soon as I saw him, I knew something was wrong. He was bluish instead of nice and pink like I remember you girls. He didn't cry or breathe. They rushed him away and worked and worked on him. At last he started breathing. But the doctor says his heart is abnormal. He suspects it is seriously malformed. If he lives long enough, they may be able to do surgery. But at this point, there isn't much hope."

Marilyn opened her mouth to ask a question, but her chest was too tight. She could not say a word. Tears welled up in Twila's dark eyes.

Suzanne jerked the ties of her pink robe. "Well, of all things. At last we get a baby boy, and then he's not all right. That doesn't seem fair to me. The Webers have had three boys in a row!" she stated vehemently.

Rita moved closer to Dad and stood in the circle of his arm. "Maybe Jesus will make him better," she whispered hopefully.

"Maybe He will," Dad smiled briefly. "Well, I wanted to tell you girls myself. I'm going to go get Aunt Faith to stay with Mother in the hospital. Michael is going to be air-lifted to St. Peter's Children's Hospital in Welbourne in about an hour. I will go with him. Aunt Julia will come over to be with you girls sometime this morning. You don't need to go to school."

When Dad said they could stay home from school, Marilyn knew he was expecting the worst. She felt sick.

"Who does the baby look like?" Twila asked softly.

"A girl would ask," Dad smiled. "Well, he has a cute little round face and reddish hair like Mother's and Marilyn's. He has just a button of a nose, of course. And he didn't open his eyes, so I don't know what color they are. They took him away so fast, we didn't get more than a glimpse. But I looked when I could, because I knew you would wonder. I wish I could give you more hope, girls. Let's pray together."

Dad sat Rita on his knee, and the other girls knelt by him. "Father in heaven," Dad prayed, "we thank You for Michael. We love him and want to take care of him. If it is Your will, Father, restore him to health so he can be a healthy baby boy." Dad's voice broke. For a moment it was very quiet. Then he continued, "But we commit him to You. Help us not to be troubled about whether this is fair. We trust Your goodness. If he must suffer, take him to Yourself. Be with Mother, and comfort her today. Be with the girls and help them to trust You. In Jesus' name, Amen."

Dad stood up. "Girls, I must leave if I'm to go with Michael. Be sweet, and cooperate with Aunt Julia."

After he left, the house seemed very empty. Rita began to cry. Marilyn led her to the couch, and they curled up together under Mother's granny afghan. Twila and Suzanne sat on the floor by their feet.

"Well, I'm so disappointed," Suzanne sighed heavily. "But surely God will heal Michael. He can, you know."

"Of course, He can," Twila said brightening a little. "And doctors can do all kinds of things to people nowadays. I think they will figure something out, maybe even give him a new heart or something."

"Michael Alex," Rita whispered. "I like that. Mother and Daddy chose a better name than any we thought up. I can hardly wait to hold him and call him Michael."

Marilyn's throat tightened. Would her little sister ever be able to hold her baby brother? She wanted so much to believe everything would come out all right. But babies did die. She remembered seeing about two dozen graves with small headstones in a little corner of the cemetery where Grandpa Hammond was buried. A sign said *Babyland*.

Please, God, she whispered in her heart, *let us keep Michael. We want him so much.*

Perhaps she ought to prepare the girls for the worst. Or was it better to give them hope?

Marilyn didn't know which was better. Finally she said, "If we're not going to school today, I think we'd better get dressed, eat breakfast, and do something worthwhile. That's what Mother would want us to do."

"And besides, we don't want Aunt Julia catching us in our robes at 9:00 in the morning," Twila said.

They dressed and ate cold cereal. Rita was still weepy. She whimpered over her cereal and wailed when Marilyn pulled her curly blonde hair while combing her. She did not cheer up until Aunt Julia came at 10:30. Marilyn was relieved to see her. There was something about Aunt Julia that made the world seem brighter.

"Good morning, girls," Aunt Julia said warmly. "I'm sorry I didn't get here sooner. So you have a baby brother at last! I know you are disappointed that he is having problems, but we'll hope for the best. I'm sure the Lord has our best interests in mind."

"His name is Michael Alex," Rita said happily. "We can hardly wait to see him."

"I should think so," Aunt Julia agreed. "And now what work should we be doing today?"

Marilyn looked around. Except for a few breakfast dishes, the house was in order. She thought of the greenhouse. Some of the flower beds needed weeding in preparation for annuals they would plant later. They discussed the unfinished work.

"I'll water the plants in the greenhouse," Aunt Julia decided, "and do whatever else needs doing. Maybe Suzanne can help me. I'll take the cordless telephone out with me. Marilyn, you, Twila, and Rita can start on that flower bed by the garage. It's nice and sunny there. That should help cheer you up."

Marilyn, Twila, and Rita got busy. The girls enjoyed messing in the dirt so it did not seem like hard work. Suddenly Twila disappeared. When she came back she explained, "I looked at the calendar. Did you think about it? This is Michael's birthday! Friday, May 5th, 1989!"

Marilyn smiled at her sister, but something squeezed her heart. Would this also be the date of Michael's death? Though the sun was warm on her back, she suddenly felt cold and pulled her sweater closer.

At noon Mother called. Her voice sounded sad when she talked about Baby Michael. "He's so sweet. I wanted to hold him so much, but they had to take him away. But, girls, we want to submit to whatever God wills. Let's not forget that."

34

She talked awhile longer to Marilyn and then to Aunt Julia.

The afternoon dragged by. Rita walked around with Iona under her arm. Twila and Suzanne actually wished they had gone to school, which amused Marilyn. Usually they were glad for a vacation. Aunt Julia called Mrs. Graham and asked that Marilyn be excused from coming over and explained why. Marilyn almost wished she could go, but knew the younger girls needed her.

"Let's take a walk in the woods," Twila suggested. "The spring flowers are starting to bloom."

"April showers bring May flowers," Rita said, "and May babies!"

"Silly!" Suzanne said scornfully. "But let's go. I love picking flowers."

The woods behind their backyard was full of tall oaks, a few evergreens, and some other trees the girls could not identify. There was some underbrush, but not enough to make walking difficult. Marilyn led the way, finding the easiest route, with Rita shadowing her. Rita never felt very secure in the woods. Their woods covered only a few acres. It was bordered by the road at the front, fields on two sides, and joined the Grahams' at the back. But it seemed wild and lonely to the younger girls. Marilyn loved it.

"You know what," she said, stopping so suddenly that Rita bumped into her, "we should make a path through the woods, a nice path we could walk on without getting all scratched up. We could use the string trimmer and the loppers to cut most of the brush. Dad might help with larger branches."

Marilyn's brainstorm fired the younger girls' imaginations, and they chattered happily as they wandered through the woods. Soon their hands were full of spring beauties and other unidentified flowers. It was 5:30 and their supper time when they trooped into the house.

Aunt Julia met them. One look at her face, and Marilyn knew. She felt as if someone had punched her in the stomach.

"I'm so sorry, girls," Aunt Julia faltered. "Your father just called. The baby died about an hour ago. I'm so sorry, girls."

Twila gave a whimper like a wounded animal, her dark eyes instant pools of misery.

But Suzanne's green eyes blazed. "I can't believe it! The doctors can make all those old people live longer, but they can't keep a little baby alive. I can't figure it out. They just didn't try hard enough!"

"Suzanne, don't talk like that," Aunt Julia's voice was firm. "Life and death is in the Lord's hand. He took Michael home to be with Him. We'll just trust He knows best."

With a wail, Suzanne ran into the living room and flung herself onto the couch.

It was a long evening. Dad never came home, but went to the hospital to be with Mother. Uncle Jerry brought Grandma Hammond over to spend the night, and Aunt Julia went home with him. Marilyn was glad Grandma was there. Grandma had a reassuring touch that calmed fretful Rita.

At 10:00 p.m. the night was still warm and the stars bright. Restless and weary, Marilyn sat on the porch steps trying to sort out her thoughts. She was heartbroken. *God, why did this have to happen?* she cried. Then into her sorrowing heart came the presence of God. Even while she sobbed, and tears ran through her fingers, she was comforted. At last the mosquitoes drove her back into the house.

She looked at herself in the bathroom mirror. This morning she was thirteen years old.

Tonight she felt so tired and so old. But except for traces of tears, the face looking back at her was just the same as usual. With a sigh, she went to bed. But how could she ever sleep?

Chapter 4

The House of Mourning

How does one greet a grieving mother when your own heart is breaking? Marilyn wondered. Her three younger sisters dashed out the door when they saw their car pull in about 9:00 the next morning. Marilyn's legs felt leaden. She remembered the excitement when Mother had brought home her little sisters. But there was no excitement this time—just heavy, heavy disappointment.

Dad helped Mother from the car. The younger girls trailed them into the house and met Marilyn and Grandma in the kitchen. Mother gave each of the girls a kiss.

"I'm so sorry," she whispered. "I wanted so much to bring a baby home to you."

Grandma hugged Mother. "Oh, Mary Ann,"

she cried. "I know how much it hurts."

Marilyn wondered if she was thinking of Grandpa's death, or of the little grave she had left in Pennsylvania many, many years before.

They went into the living room, and Dad settled Mother into the most comfortable chair. Mother held out her arms to Rita, just as she had done for five years. Rita stiffened. "I'm not the baby anymore," she said distinctly. "I'm not the baby anymore, and I'm not the youngest!"

Mother smiled faintly. "But Michael isn't living, and I still need my littlest one to cuddle."

Rita considered a moment, then sat on the arm of Mother's chair and rested her curly head on Mother's shoulder. Mother respected her new independence and said nothing more. She leaned back in her chair with a weary sigh.

"Well, girls," Dad said gently, "as Mother said, we are sorry we cannot bring a baby brother home for you as we had been looking forward to. God had other plans for Michael. As a family, we are not going to doubt His ways. But we hurt, and it is all right to cry. Michael is in heaven. He will never know any of the troubles of this life. He will never cry or be hungry or sick. The part of him that has feelings, that would do right or wrong, that would love us— that is with God."

Marilyn knew he was speaking simply so even Rita could understand. But she was glad. To her confused mind, Dad's uncomplicated explanation of the soul was comforting.

"Would you like to see Michael now?" Dad asked. "They suggested at the hospital that we bring him home for you girls to see. Then we need to take him to the funeral home where an autopsy is going to be done. Afterwards, the funeral director will prepare his body. Mother and I have decided we would like a small funeral here at home tomorrow."

"Autopsy? What is that?" Suzanne wondered.

"The doctor wants to know exactly what was wrong with Michael's heart. Some specially-trained men are going to open up his chest, kind of like surgery, to see what they can find out. Maybe they will learn something that will help some other little baby who is born with a heart that isn't normal."

"Do you have Michael here?" Twila asked.

Dad nodded. He got up and went outside. When he came back in, he was carrying a small white box. He took off the top and lovingly lifted out his small son, snugly wrapped in a hospital

41

blanket. He handed the baby to Marilyn.

She was a bit frightened. She had never touched a dead person's body. She expected him to be hard and cold. But he wasn't. He was as soft and cuddly as a live baby. But there was no life. She unwrapped the blanket and looked at his tiny body, perfectly formed. His skin was bluish, and his lips and fingernails were almost purple. Long blonde eyelashes fanned out on his soft cheeks. Soft reddish down covered his head. He was so cute. With a sigh, she handed him to Twila.

Twila took him eagerly. She seemed transported from reality. She cuddled his soft, limp body. She put him up to her shoulder. She patted him. She wrapped and unwrapped his blanket. She crooned softly to him. Love and longing were in her every motion.

Grandma gave a strangled, choking sob, and Twila looked up, startled. In an instant she was back to heartbreaking reality. Tears welled up in her eyes and ran down her cheeks. She clung to the baby as if she would never let him go. At last Dad gently took the small bundle and let Suzanne and Rita each have a turn holding him. Grandma and Mother each held him awhile, then Dad took him. After cuddling him a moment, he laid Michael tenderly back in the box.

Dad and Grandma helped Mother to the bedroom, then Dad took the box which held Michael and left for the funeral home.

All morning people kept stopping in. They brought food and said kind and comforting words to the girls, Grandma, and Aunt Faith who had come to help. Mother was resting.

After Dad returned, they ate a lunch someone brought. Uncle Jerry came, and he and Dad went out to the garage to make the casket. Dad did not like the expensive caskets the funeral home sold. "I will make a casket for my son," he said firmly. Marilyn knew that was Dad's way. There was nothing else he could do for Michael, except make his casket. He would consider it an honor.

It was quiet in the house. Rita sat on the front porch holding Iona. Marilyn could not see what comfort she got out of a chicken. Twila complained about it to Aunt Faith. "What will people think? There Rita sits, holding a chicken and stroking its feathers. It's so embarrassing. They'll probably think she's not normal."

"It is normal for a little girl," Aunt Faith said firmly. "She finds comfort in that chicken. It's her way of coping when the going gets rough—and her world is upset right now. If the chicken helps, let her alone."

Twila stood still in the middle of the room. Suddenly she turned and fled to her bedroom, sobbing, "I guess I need a chicken too!" Grandma followed to comfort her. When they didn't return for a long while, Marilyn suspected they had both fallen asleep.

Dad had asked Suzanne to bring her life-size baby doll to the garage to get the measurements for the casket. She had stayed with Dad and Uncle Jerry. She was like Dad. She found comfort in doing something, even if it was nothing more than sitting on a pail and watching.

Marilyn needed time alone. It was cloudy and cool, so she put on a jacket and scarf and stepped outside. Without conscious thought, her feet took her toward the woods. Yesterday seemed so long ago. Remembering their exciting plan, she tried to figure out a natural route through the woods. Having nothing to mark the path, she gave up and picked a variety of flowers instead. Somehow that was soothing.

She found the little plot of Dutchmen's-breeches they had discovered the day before.

Rita had called them Grandpa Pants in her funny little way of saying things wrong.

Marilyn sat on a large granite rock and thought about her family. They had had such a peaceful, ordinary existence up until now. Why couldn't it have kept on that way? They would have loved Michael so much. They had not even gotten to know him as a real person. It hardly seemed fair. Yet Dad said they were not going to doubt God's wisdom. She knew Dad was right and felt safe with his decision.

On their dining room wall hung a motto where it could be easily seen at every meal. It said, *All things work together for good to them that love God. Romans 8:28.* At lunch, Grandma had pointed to it. "That's for us," she had said. "Good can come even when we're hurting." Though Marilyn's heart ached, God was near.

Suddenly Marilyn thought of Nancy Graham. No wonder the poor woman was so bitter. She did not believe in a comforting God. She did not believe in a loving Saviour. When trouble came, she had nothing to cling to.

Marilyn looked at the flowers in her hand. Suddenly she turned and ran through the woods, across the yard, and into the kitchen.

45

"Aunt Faith, may I ride my bike over to the Grahams' and take these flowers to Mrs. Graham?"

Aunt Faith knew about Nancy Graham. She smiled. "You have learned something valuable if you can share with others when you are sorrowing yourself," she said. "Ask your father, and I'll help you get the flowers ready."

With Dad's approval, Aunt Faith carefully wet the flower stems with paper towels and put the bouquet in a plastic bag with holders to hook over the handlebars. In a short time Marilyn was at the Grahams'. Mr. Graham was not home so Marilyn let herself into the house, calling so Mrs. Graham would not be frightened.

"I've brought you some spring flowers that grow in our woods," Marilyn said.

Mrs. Graham reached out eagerly for the bouquet. In that moment, Marilyn began to understand what Mrs. Graham was missing. A naturalist would love being outdoors among trees and flowers. Mrs. Graham's handicap kept her inside.

Her large hands touched the dainty flowers reverently. "Bloodroots, violets, spring beauties," she murmured. "And this is a hepatica, but they are probably about over with. And Dutchmen's-breeches. Aren't they fascinating little things! Soon the trilliums will be blooming. Springtime is so wonderful. Thank you for bringing me these flowers, Marilyn. It's probably all the springtime I will get."

Marilyn got a vase out of the cupboard and placed the flowers on the stand beside Mrs. Graham's recliner.

"Is there anything I can do for you while I'm here?" Marilyn asked.

Mrs. Graham looked up. "No, I don't think so. Really, I'm surprised you're here. What brought you? I thought your family was mourning. Didn't your baby brother die?"

Marilyn flinched. Mrs. Graham's voice didn't have the tender concern Marilyn had heard from friends stopping by their house.

"I wanted to bring you flowers," Marilyn stammered. How could she tell Mrs. Graham she wanted to comfort her because she didn't understand the love of God like they did at home? "And, yes, my baby brother died."

"Something was wrong with his heart, wasn't there? You can be glad he didn't live. Sickly babies are an awful nuisance. Awfully expensive too. We had a baby years ago. She

47

died. Lived only a few months. I didn't waste my time mourning, but Bob sure did."

The cold, heartless words sent chills of horror through Marilyn. Her cheeks flushed as anger surged through her. Her thumping heart filled her chest till she could hardly breathe. One part of her wanted to run out of the house and never come back. Another part wanted to tell Nancy Graham exactly how wicked she was, and how God would surely punish her if she did not change her bitter ways.

Marilyn's eyes dropped to the flowers, and she remembered it was God's love that had caused her to bring them. "Well, we love our baby and wanted to keep him. But we believe God knows best. We believe Michael is in heaven with God. And someday we can see him again. Your baby is in heaven too."

Mrs. Graham snorted scornfully. "I suppose it's comforting to believe that stuff, but I don't. My baby would have made a pitiful angel. Maybe your brother is prettier."

Hurt and dismay choked Marilyn. Without another word, she fled out the door, leaped onto her bike, and sped home. She never wanted to see Nancy Graham again.

When she got home, they were all gathered

in the dining room. The little casket, so lovingly built by Dad and Uncle Jerry, was sitting on the table.

"Will it be all right?" Dad asked Marilyn anxiously. She touched the satin-smooth wood. It was made of pine the color of clover honey. It looked like it belonged to a tiny baby. "Yes," she said, "but we must pad it with something soft. Mother has some quilt batting we can put in the bottom."

"And we can line it with the afghan Mother made for him and snuggle him in it," Twila added eagerly.

Dad was pleased. "Well, I'll leave that to you women," he said. "And I did think it would be nice if Michael's name was engraved on the casket lid. I called Sue and asked if she would bring her engraving tool over. She should be here any time. I need to go get Michael now. He should be ready."

Sue came. She had a pretty, artistic handwriting, and by the time Dad returned with the baby, she had engraved Michael's name on the inside of the casket lid.

"If no one minds," Mother smiled apologetically, "Aunt Julia and I will get Michael ready alone." Aunt Julia lifted the little casket and carried it to the bedroom. Mother followed with the afghan and quietly closed the door.

After awhile Mother called the family in. The sewing machine cabinet was covered with a pale blue sheet Mother had bought to make curtains. The casket was sitting on it. The afghan lined the casket and hung over the sides. Little Michael lay like a sleeping baby, one tiny hand against his cheek, and the other at his side. He was wearing the tiny blue sleeper Mother had planned for the baby to wear home if it was a boy. A hush fell over the group, almost as if they were afraid to wake him up.

At last they left the silent little form and went to eat the supper no one cared about. They ate because Aunt Julia had brought it, and because it was just the usual thing to do.

Marilyn ate quickly and returned to the bedroom. She wanted to be alone with Michael. She traced her finger over the engraving on the casket lid.

Michael Alex Hammond

She liked the name Mother and Dad had chosen for their son. But he would never write it. It would never be scrawled at the top of his school papers, engraved on the front of his

50

Bible, printed on his baptismal and wedding certificates, or signed on a check. His name would only be used by them to identify a son and brother who had been here . . . and now was gone.

But he was with Jesus, and that was what mattered most. The thought comforted Marilyn.

Chapter 5

Laid to Rest

For Mother's sake, a family funeral was planned for the next day, which was Sunday. Dad and Mother didn't want to leave out the church family, so an invitation was sent on the Church Call Line inviting them to a viewing at the Hammond home, from seven to nine o'clock Saturday evening.

Michael's casket remained in Mother and Dad's large bedroom. Mother sat in a comfortable chair by the bedroom door. Marilyn settled on the edge of the bed near Mother, but the younger girls wandered forlornly about. Dad welcomed the families as they came into the room. After expressing their love and sympathy, and viewing the tiny baby, people went out to the living room to visit with others before leaving.

Marilyn was strangely comforted by how much people cared. They had never known Michael, but they understood he was a real baby, loved and longed for by the Hammond family. The women embraced mother and wept. The men wrung Dad's hand sympathetically. Marilyn supposed they thought of their own children and grandchildren. A few may have remembered other small graves.

Uncle Jerry, Aunt Julia, and Ricky came, bringing along Consuela, the little Mexican girl that had once stolen things from their Christian day school. She often stayed with them when her folks grew tired of her and her Grandmother Weatherby was unable to keep her. For once Ricky had nothing to say. He and Consuela stood side by side and solemnly viewed the baby. Marilyn wondered what they were thinking.

Consuela turned to Mother. "I have a baby brother too," she said, "but my mother doesn't like him. He cries too much. His name is Roberto." A pained expression crossed Mother's face.

A tiny tot wandered back after her family had gone through. She stood on tiptoe trying to see into the casket. Dad picked her up and let her see Michael. She looked and looked, then struggled to get down. She left, only to return again. Three times Dad picked her up to see Michael. She was fascinated by this sleeping baby everyone came to see, but no one picked up or cuddled.

Marilyn felt so sorry for Dad. Dad loved his daughters. They never doubted it. But she knew fathers long for sons. Dad would have loved to do with Michael all the things only fathers and sons do together. Instead, there was this quiet little form in a tiny, homemade casket. He hovered over it in a way that said, "This is my son. My son Michael Alex Hammond. By the will of God, he is not alive, but he is still my son, and I love him."

Aunt Bess, Uncle Will, and Markie came into the bedroom. Markie looked at the baby for a long time, then turned to Marilyn. "Don't cry, Marilyn," he said simply. "Mama said your baby is with Jesus."

Marilyn had not been crying, but these tender words from her Down's syndrome cousin brought tears to her eyes and a tightness to her throat. As usual, Markie caught the things of the spirit, even though his understanding was limited in other ways.

At last the people were all gone, except for

Aunt Faith, Uncle Nathan, Sue, and her older sister. They tidied up the house, then they left too.

Marilyn was completely worn out. Her head throbbed, and her legs ached. She could not understand why. She had hardly done any work all day. Mother looked exhausted, and Rita was whimpering in that irritating way she had when it was far past her bedtime.

Dad carried the little casket down to a cool corner in the basement. When he returned, he said, "We're tired. Grief is more tiring than hard work. We've hardly been alone all day. Let's gather in the living room, pray together, and then go to bed."

Dad encouraged each of them to trust God and His wisdom in taking Michael from this life. He explained the funeral service and asked the girls if they had any questions. Then he led in prayer, earnestly asking God for strength for the coming day.

Marilyn went to bed comforted.

The next morning, a robin was singing in the oak outside Marilyn's window when she awoke. Sunshine was streaming through her east window, slanting warm shafts of light across her bed. For a moment she lay in perfect peace and contentment, enjoying the promise of a lovely spring day. Then she remembered—this was the day they would bury the little brother they had wanted for so long. A heavy weight seemed to press down on her chest. Abruptly she rolled over and crushed her face into the pillow, trying to shut out the knowledge and the pain.

Later, Twila's voice came to her. "You'd better get up and dress, Marilyn. Dad said we are going to church this morning. Grandma Hammond is coming over to stay with Mother while we're gone. I asked him if I could stay home too, but he said no. He said we need the people of God now more than we ever did."

Marilyn was not surprised Dad felt that way. That was how Dad was. Slowly she got dressed and went to the kitchen. She set out cereal, milk, and juice, while Twila set the table.

Grandma came, and they went to church. The girls sat with Aunt Julia. There was something about her loving presence that helped them through the touching service. Brother Don preached on suffering and death and the bliss of heaven. It was almost like a funeral service even though there was no casket there. Marilyn noticed some of the women weeping.

They left soon after the service. Some of the church women were bringing in a large meal because all the Hammonds who could come would be there. Most of Mother's relatives lived too far away to come on such short notice, but Uncle James and Aunt Danette and their children were coming. They lived only an hour and a half away.

Marilyn was helping in the kitchen when Dad called for her to come to the front door. Bob Graham was standing there. He was holding a large arrangement of flowers in a vase. "These are for you, Marilyn. Nancy sent me to the florist to get them. Usually she isn't much for fancy flowers. She likes those she can grow herself or find in the wilds, but she wanted to express her sympathy. And she apologizes for talking so thoughtlessly to you. She is worried that you won't come back."

Marilyn was embarrassed. "I shouldn't have run off like that," she confessed. "I guess I was upset. I'm sorry. I'll be back when Mother doesn't need me anymore."

"We'd sure appreciate it if you would. Your Dad said maybe your cousin Sue could come for awhile until your Mother is back on her feet." Marilyn nodded. She thought it was a good idea.

Mr. Graham shifted uncomfortably, "I'm just wanting to say myself, that you folks sure have my sympathy. We had a baby ourselves, about 16 years ago. I named her Nanette. She was the cutest little thing. Looked like a China baby. The doctor said she wasn't normal, and called her a Mongoloid. They have some other fancy name for that now. There was a problem with her heart, and she wouldn't eat right. After two months she died. I thought I couldn't stand it, but Nancy was kind of cold, and said it was a good thing. Said she'd have been a bother anyway, it being sickly and retarded, and all that. Afterwards Nancy never took much interest in babies. All she thought about was trees and bushes and flowers and that sort of thing. I like nature too, but I'd rather have had the babies." He sighed wistfully.

"Come in and see Michael," Dad suggested warmly.

"No, no, I don't want to intrude. But you certainly have my sympathy."

Marilyn felt sorry for Mr. Graham. And though she couldn't understand why, she felt sorry for Mrs. Graham too. It probably was not easy for Mr. Graham to live with her. She was a hard woman and unhappy, and now even her enjoyment of nature was being denied her. Marilyn could see why she acted as she did.

"Thank you for the flowers," Marilyn said. "They are lovely."

She carried the bouquet of gladiolus and ferns inside and set them on a stand in the living room. They added a cheerful note to the house.

The family gathered for dinner. Then later, while the table was being cleared, those wanting to could go into the bedroom to see Michael before the service.

Marilyn sat where she had the evening before. She saw her cousins Jeff and Steve Hammond come into the room. Jeff was so tall and manly that sometimes Marilyn was almost afraid of him. At fifteen he suddenly seemed much older than she. But when he turned away, Marilyn saw tears in his dark eyes. Steve, thirteen like herself, had grown too, and no longer looked pudgy.

After looking at Michael, he came to Marilyn. "I'm so sorry," he blurted. "I know you've been looking forward to a baby. And it's worse, being a boy and all. I mean, well, girls are all right, but you've been needing a boy . . . and now he's dead." He stood miserably before her. Marilyn almost felt she should say something to comfort him, but he turned abruptly and left the room.

Barry Martin, a cousin just a year older than Marilyn, had seen Michael the evening before. But he had come again. Before he left, he turned soberly to Marilyn. "You know," he said, "I never thought before how precious babies are. Sometimes I get mad at Janet and Philip and Molly and don't treat them like I should. I never thought about them dying when they were babies, and we'd never really have gotten to know them. I'd miss them something awful now. I . . . I just never thought!"

He left. Marilyn began to see how some good could come from losing Michael. Maybe other folks would think about how precious babies are, like Barry had.

When everyone that wanted to had seen Michael for the last time, Dad and Mother called the girls in. "Girls," Dad said huskily, "the time has come to say good-by to Michael's body. You may touch him if you like."

Marilyn looked down at her baby brother. She had slipped in alone earlier and touched his cool little cheek and tucked her finger into the curve of his tiny hand. Of course, there had been no responding tug. It broke her heart. She did not want to do it again. She reached down and ran her fingers over the soft down of his auburn hair. It was the only thing about him that did not feel of death.

The other girls shook their heads mutely. Mother took the afghan and smoothed it tenderly over him until only his sweet little face showed. And then with trembling fingers, she covered his face too.

"Good-by, Michael," Dad said softly and closed the lid. Placing screws in the pre-drilled holes, he began fastening shut the lid. His hands fumbled at times with the screwdriver. Marilyn thought it took awfully long. At last he picked up the casket, carried it to the dining room, and placed it on a table pushed against the wall.

Chairs had been placed in rows in the living and dining room, and all the relatives were seated. Marilyn's family found places reserved for them.

Brother Don was in charge of the service. After the Shepherd Psalm, he read the obituary Mother had written. Then he opened his Bible to 2 Samuel 12:23 and briefly told the story of David's sorrow over the death of his baby son. Brother Don emphasized David's words, "I shall go to him, but he shall not return to me."

He spoke tenderly to each of them. "Alex," he said to Dad, "even though you are going to miss the joy of having a son to follow in your steps, live nobly for the sake of your wife and daughters. Be as good an example to them in coping with sorrow as you have been in joy."

He turned to Mother. "Mary Ann," he said gently, "a mother's grief is deep and not soon forgotten, but trust in the Saviour. He knows and understands. He'll give you the comfort and courage to go on."

There were tears in his eyes as he looked at the four sisters. "Girls," he said, "you are disappointed, and it hurts. Death is hard to understand. But determine now to live for Jesus, and someday you can meet your brother in heaven."

His message touched their hearts deeply. They wept tears of hurt, grief, and submission. Marilyn thought she would never forget his kind words. Mother handed the girls tissues, noticing their needs even in her own grief.

Dad knew how difficult it would be for the family to sing together, so he had asked three of the church girls to sing. They stood out of sight in the hallway and sang, *My Ways are*

Higher Than Your Ways, and *God Holds My Hand.* The sweet singing and comforting words encouraged Marilyn.

Dad stood. "Thank you for coming and sharing in our grief," he said simply. After Brother Don led in a closing prayer, everyone filed out quietly and left for the cemetery.

Marilyn and her family rode in Uncle Nathan's van. The little casket was tucked between the two front seats. On the way Dad tied macramé cords to two eyebolts fastened to the casket. They would be used to lower it into the ground.

At the cemetery the undertaker led them to Babyland. The casket was set upon two narrow boards lying across the open grave. After a short meditation and a fitting poem, Brother Don read the committal, "For as it has pleased Almighty God to take out of this world the soul of Michael Hammond, we commit the body to the ground; earth to earth, dust to dust, and commit the soul to God who gave it, looking for the resurrection and the life to come through our Lord Jesus Christ."

Marilyn felt choked up. The spring air was fresh, but she could hardly breathe. One part of her was glad to be part of a family that could have a reverent and meaningful funeral. Another part of her screamed silently that it was awful to put their dear baby in that small, dark hole and cover him with dirt.

But the boards were removed, and Uncle Tim and Uncle James lowered the casket out of sight. Dad picked up a shovelful of dirt, carefully spilled it into the hole, and handed the shovel to Uncle Nathan. Stepping back, Dad put his arm around Mother. One by one, other men and boys took turns until the grave was filled.

Marilyn glanced at the undertaker. There was a look of respectful wonder on his face. She supposed he had never seen anything like this service. But then, neither had she. Never before had she been at a baby's funeral. Grandpa Hammond's funeral had been more formal.

Marilyn and her sisters wandered through Babyland, fascinated by the grave markers. Most of the stones were shades of pink or blue or white and engraved with angels and flowers and lambs. Most of the dates declared the graves' occupants were no more than five years old. Each marker had a touching story to tell. They were the last ones to leave the cemetery.

"Babyland is a sad, sad place," Twila said

softly. "Think of all the sad mothers."

Marilyn thought of the mothers and fathers, brothers and sisters, and grandparents who must have wept over these graves. She wondered if the hurt ever went away.

"Well, at least all these children went to heaven," Suzanne said confidently. "There are probably some real sinners over in the other part of the cemetery."

Marilyn sighed. Suzanne could be so blunt.

As they left the cemetery, Marilyn looked back. All she could see now was the dark mound of fresh earth against the green spring grass. Though his body was returned to the clay from which he came, Michael's soul had gone back to God.

Chapter 6

Going On

"I feel all mixied inside," Rita said mournfully the next morning, stirring her cornflakes into an unappetizing mess.

"Mixied?" repeated Twila with a wan smile. "I guess that says it right, but I think you mean, all-mixed-up. Do we have to go to school, Dad?"

"Doesn't Mother need our help?" Marilyn asked hopefully.

"I know how you feel," Dad said gently. "But we have to get on with our lives, and that means school for you girls. In just a few weeks school will be out, and then you can be home with Mother. I think I'll work nearer home and drop in at lunch for awhile until we see how Mother gets along. Aunt Faith is coming over this morning to do the laundry. I'll stay home today and see what needs to be done in the greenhouse and gardens."

Mother was not feeling well, so the girls whispered good-bye at the bedroom door. Then Dad took them to school. "See you this evening, girls," he said as they climbed from the car.

It was a long day. Rita was weepy on the way home from school. Marilyn felt like crying along with her. Twila was in one of her silent moods, as if she were in a different world. Suzanne was as cross as could be. Aunt Faith chattered cheerfully, but when none of the girls responded, she grew silent. Soon they were home.

Every evening that week a family from church brought in supper. On Friday Suzanne chortled, "Special food every night, and not a thing I didn't like!"

Marilyn was glad for the food. Otherwise she or Dad would have had to prepare the meals. She still wasn't too good at cooking, and Dad's cooking meant hot dogs and applesauce, with ice cream for dessert.

Every day after school the younger girls raced to the mailbox to see how many sympathy cards there were. Marilyn suspected Dad and Mother deliberately left the mail in the box so the girls could enjoy getting it. By the end of the first week, there were several cards in the box every day.

"I didn't know people loved us this much," Suzanne said in an awed voice. She held up a card. "Whoever are Myron and Alice Chupp, Mother?"

"She is a lady I grew up with," Mother answered. "She lost a baby too, only theirs was ten months old."

"At least they had their baby that long," Suzanne observed. "Why did God give us Michael, Mother, if He was going to let him die anyway? If we hadn't known about Michael, it wouldn't have hurt so to lose him. We didn't even get to know him," she said indignantly.

Marilyn wondered how Suzanne always managed to say so bluntly what the rest of them only felt vaguely and could never quite put into words. Mother smiled sadly. "Remember, we are not to question God's ways, Suzanne. And there is another way to look at Michael's birth. We studied a poem when I was in school. A couple lines from it say, 'Tis better to have loved and lost, than never to have loved at all.' "

Twila looked up with interest. "Say that again, Mother. What does it mean?"

" 'Tis better to have loved and lost, than

never to have loved at all,' " Mother repeated. "That means every time we love someone, we are blessed in some way or other, even if later something happens to the relationship. Perhaps the person dies, moves away, or the friendship may even be broken by unhappy circumstances. Whatever the case, knowing and loving the person was still valuable. And we loved Michael, even if it was for such a short time."

Though her younger sisters didn't understand, Twila's face brightened. "I think I know what you mean, Mother. Just think what we would have missed if we would never have had Michael at all!"

The thought thrilled Marilyn too. "We did enjoy planning for him, Mother, all of us together. And we found out how much people care about us, not just our relatives, but the church people, and even that Chupp family you knew years ago. And I think I want to go to heaven more than I ever did before."

There were tears in Mother's eyes. "Sometimes I forget the blessings too, in wishing we could have kept Michael. But, girls, let's try to see the blessings. They are there."

"Another thing," Suzanne blurted again. "You said we could go to James' Bible & Book

Store to pick out birth announcements after the baby was born, and we knew whether it was a boy or girl. Now we don't get to!"

"Oh, be quiet, Suzanne," Twila said sharply. "What can't be helped, can't be helped."

They all sat quietly for a while. "Well, I suppose we could send out birth and death announcements," Mother said thoughtfully. "Get me a piece of typing paper, Suzanne."

Mother folded the piece of paper greeting-card style. On the outside she wrote carefully, *In Memory of Michael Alex Hammond.* Inside she wrote Michael's date of birth and death, his weight and measurements, and then all their names, much as in a regular birth announcement.

"And now let me draw some pictures on the front," Twila begged enthusiastically.

"Very well," Mother agreed, "then we'll show it to Dad and see how he feels about it. If he approves, perhaps he can take it to school and make copies. If we're going to do it, they should be mailed soon."

Twila took the announcement and disappeared. When she didn't return, Marilyn went to find her. She found Twila sitting on the floor in the room that would have been Michael's,

71

carefully drawing butterflies, birds, and flowers just as she had done on the little white crib.

Marilyn sat down heavily in the rocker. She had not been in the room since Michael had come and gone. The door had always been closed. It hurt to see the empty crib; the dresser full of baby clothes; the diaper stacker; and the powder, lotion, and baby wipes on the dressing table.

Twila finished and handed the announcement to Marilyn. "Is it good enough, do you think?" she asked anxiously.

Marilyn looked at it. "It's lovely, Twila," she said.

"It's the only thing I can ever do for Michael," Twila said in a choked whisper. Suddenly she started to sob. Marilyn drew Twila's head onto her lap, put her arms around her, and cried with her. While she wept for her own disappointment, Marilyn realized she was also weeping for Twila's. Twila was always a dreamer. Now one of her happiest dreams was shattered.

"Someday the hurt will go away," Marilyn said hopefully. "That's what folks said that came to see us."

"Well, if it doesn't, I don't think I can stand it much longer," Twila mourned.

Later on, the girls wiped their tears and went to show the announcement to Mother and Dad. Dad promised to make copies.

One day Marilyn was opening sympathy cards. "Why, Mother, see here!" she exclaimed. "This card has money in it. Why would someone give us money?"

"Perhaps they thought we had unusual expenses when Michael was born, or perhaps for funeral expenses," Mother said. "Who is it from, Marilyn?"

"It is from your Uncle Maynard, Mother. I thought you said they were poor, with Aunt Cynthia being in the hospital so often. One time we even sent them money," Marilyn remembered.

Tears came to Mother's eyes. "How like them!" she murmured. "Always thinking of others, even with so little themselves. Marilyn, you'll often find folks who have had trouble themselves are the quickest to help others."

Several more sympathy cards contained money. "We should get a grave marker before too long," Dad said thoughtfully. "Maybe we'll use the money for that. The hospital expenses were not much more than expected, and the funeral expenses were low because we took care of most of the details ourselves. Yes, that's what we'll do."

Not many evenings later, a man with a briefcase knocked on their door. "Good evening," he said respectfully. "I'm Jack Smith, and I'm certainly sorry to hear about your baby son's death. If you would have a few minutes, I can show you some information about grave markers."

Dad invited him in, and they all gathered around the dining room table. Mr. Smith described the different kinds of stone used for grave markers. Some even came from other parts of the world and cost a fortune.

"But I know you folks aren't interested in those," he said at last. "I'll show you some more reasonable markers."

He laid open a display of simple children's markers. Marilyn thought instantly of Babyland. The girls would have chosen the blue-gray marker, but Dad liked the soft gray one best. The girls were allowed to choose the decorative engraving and selected one with a little lamb in one corner and birds and flowers in the other. Michael's name and birth and death date would be engraved on it.

"Whatever you all like is fine with me," Mother said wearily. It was necessary to choose a marker. It was also painful.

The man wrote down their exact specifications.

"We like to think this kind of decision over awhile before giving the final go-ahead," Dad said firmly. "We'll discuss it, then if we're still convinced this is what we want, I'll sign this paper and send it to you with the payment. We can install the marker ourselves."

"That's fine," said Mr. Smith. "And after we have the contract, we'll deliver the gravestone to your door within six weeks."

Dad checked about markers at a few other places, but found nothing more suitable. They sent off the contract that Mr. Smith had left with them. The girls were pleased and excited. A grave marker was one last thing the family could do in memory of Michael.

Chapter 7

Happiness Returns

"Well, now that school's out, maybe we can relax and think once!" Suzanne stated as the Hammond family got up from devotions early one morning in June.

"What!" Dad exclaimed. "You're saying you didn't think in school? I thought that's mainly what you're there for!"

"Oh, I know," the little girl giggled, "but that's hard thinking. I'm ready for some easy thinking."

Marilyn smiled. Suzanne did not find book learning easy. "Is it *easy thinking* to help me plant pepper plants?" Marilyn asked. "Dad says that's what we're doing this morning."

Suzanne grinned mischievously and replied, "That's my kind of thinking. I like messing in the dirt, ' specially on a nice morning like this!"

Dad left for his carpenter work, Mother started the laundry, and Twila and Rita did the dishes. Marilyn and Suzanne went merrily out into the lovely morning sunshine.

Their family had never meant to be produce growers, but somehow neighborhood folks, and even passing tourists, would see Mother's large, lovely garden and stop to ask about vegetables. Mother's garden got bigger and bigger till now even Dad was involved, sometimes staying home from work to see that things got done. They had planned to plant less this year because of the new baby, but when their hopes were buried in a small plot in Babyland, Marilyn noticed Dad planted another patch of potatoes and one of corn.

Marilyn thought about their family as she dug eighteen holes and set the sturdy pepper plants in them for Suzanne to plant. To her surprise, the hurt of losing Michael had lessened. Sometimes, like this morning, Dad teased a bit as he used to. They had smiled, and life had seemed bright and good. The stabbing pain of grief that had made her feel tired and old had softened to a dull ache. Sometimes she almost forgot it was there.

Once she and her sisters had been laughing at something, and suddenly Twila had looked stricken and said, "Oh, we shouldn't be laughing when our baby just died."

Dad had stated gently, "It is all right to cry when we are grieving, but it is also right to be happy when the hurt starts to go away. Laugh, girls, as long as you aren't being silly. Mother and I like to see our girls happy."

Marilyn knew what Suzanne meant about wanting to relax and think. Michael's death and finishing school had occupied so much of their thoughts that somehow they needed some slow family living to piece their lives back together. Thankfully, the whole summer stretched before them. Marilyn was glad.

"Too bad peppers don't taste better than they do," Suzanne remarked as she tucked the dirt around the last plant. "These plants surely look nice, and the peppers are so pretty when they're ready to pick."

"I like peppers to eat fresh, and they're good in hot dishes too," Marilyn declared.

"Well, I can eat them," Suzanne said, "but just barely! What I like are radishes and little green onions."

Suzanne wandered off to the spring garden.

Marilyn saw her sitting in the shade of the maple tree eating fresh radishes and onions, rubbing the dirt off on her dress. Marilyn wondered how much dirt the younger girls ate in a year's time by eating vegetables straight from the garden. Well, they didn't use pesticides, and everyone was healthy. She guessed that was what mattered.

Marilyn, Twila, Suzanne, and Rita all weeded in the pea patch the rest of the morning. The peas were already creeping up the woven wire fence, so this would be the last time the weeds could be pulled. Soon the peas would be blooming and then would come the fascinating but back-tiring job of picking the plump pods. Marilyn and her sisters all liked to eat peas straight from the garden. Peas were also their favorite winter vegetable. With that in mind, there was a sense of satisfaction as they pulled the last of the weeds and dumped them onto the compost pile.

Later in the afternoon, Mother handed Marilyn a loaf of fresh bread. "Take this along when you go over to the Grahams," she said.

"Oh, Mother, do I have to?" Marilyn objected.

Mother was surprised. "Why not? I baked this small loaf just for them."

"How do you know they even like homemade bread? Bob brings bread home from the store every few days. It's nice, white bread."

Mother looked a bit hurt but unconvinced. "I did put some brown flour in the bread like I often do, but I'm sure they won't mind that. If Mrs. Graham doesn't like homemade bread, I venture to say Mr. Graham will. He said as much to Dad once at work."

Reluctantly Marilyn took the loaf and carefully placed it in the basket of her bicycle. If she had to take bread, she didn't want it to be smashed bread.

For several weeks Sue had worked for the Grahams, but now Marilyn went over every afternoon. To her surprise, she had been glad to see Mrs. Graham, and Mrs. Graham had seemed glad to see her.

Marilyn let herself into the house. Mrs. Graham was in her recliner as usual. Marilyn handed her the loaf of bread. "It's from Mother," she said. "She baked it just this morning."

Mrs. Graham held the perfect loaf of bread almost reverently in her large hands. "Why, that's wonderful!" she said. "Tell your mother I appreciate it. Take it into the kitchen, cut me the heel, spread it with butter, and bring it to me. I don't want to wait until this evening."

Marilyn did as she was told, and then went out to sweep off the sidewalks and do the other outside jobs on Bob's list. When she came back in, Mrs. Graham called to her. "Marilyn, that bread reminded me of my grandmother. I haven't thought of her for years. She was the old-fashioned kind, a lot like you folks. She went to church, sewed her own dresses, raised chickens, had a big garden patch, and baked her own brown bread. It tasted just like your mother's.

"I know she loved me, but she didn't approve of me much. When I told her I was going to be a naturalist she said she had no doubt I could be a very good naturalist. But she said she didn't think I'd make a very good woman. I wasn't quite sure what she meant, but it made me mad."

Mrs. Graham brooded for awhile, and Marilyn dusted the room while she waited to be dismissed. Mrs. Graham's moods could shift with no warning. It paid to be cautious.

"I think she was right," Nancy suddenly snapped vehemently. "I'm not a very good woman. And now I'm not a good naturalist either. I guess I'm not really a good anything.

Marilyn, I think your mother is teaching you to be a good woman. Go home and learn to make bread like she does. Learn all the other things too. Good-bye, I'll see you tomorrow."

As she guided her bike down the country road, Marilyn thought about what Mrs. Graham had said about good bread and being a good woman. She was ashamed that she had been embarrassed about Mother's brown bread. The bread had made Mrs. Graham reveal more of herself than anything else had done. She would tell Mother about it. And she would long remember the things Nancy Graham had said.

A few mornings later, Rita came in from the chicken house weeping. In her arms she carried her brown chicken, its bloodied head flopping lifelessly as she stumbled up the steps.

"What have we here?" Dad asked, setting down his toolbox and putting a compassionate hand on the little girl's shoulder.

"It's Iona. She was just lying there plumb dead. Oh, Daddy, how come she died?"

"Yuk!" Twila exclaimed. "Put her down, Rita. You'll get blood all over yourself. Go throw her over the fence."

"I will not!" Rita wailed. "Oh, my poor chicken. First we lost our baby, and now we lose

Iona! Oh, what made her dead, Daddy?"

Marilyn felt impatient. "What a fuss over a chicken, Rita. Imagine putting Michael and Iona in the same category! Babies are more important than chickens."

"We could do an autopsy, Dad, and find out what made her die," Suzanne grinned thoughtlessly.

"Girls, be kind," Dad said. "Rita, I think a weasel must have killed Iona. This is how weasels kill. Tonight I will have to carefully check the chicken house and see how it got in, or it will kill more chickens. I'm terribly sorry it got your pet, Rita. I know you'll miss Iona."

"Lay her behind the garage, Rita," Mother said, giving the sad little girl a hug. "Perhaps later someone can bury her."

With a sniff and a sigh, Rita carried her pet behind the garage, then went sadly to the tire swing. As the other girls went to work in the garden, they could see her swinging slowly back and forth, singing a mournful song she made up as she sang.

Twila and Suzanne each had to weed two rows of corn every morning. Afterwards, they were sometimes free to play awhile. Marilyn was hoeing potatoes. Because she enjoyed it, she decided to keep on until Mother asked her to do something different.

About 10:30 Marilyn noticed the three younger girls beyond the far end of the garden where the woods shaded the yard. Twila had a shovel and was digging a hole between the roots of a big red oak.

They're going to bury Iona, Marilyn thought. *I can't see making such a fuss over a chicken. Now if it were a cat or dog . . . But maybe it'll help make Rita feel better.*

She worked her way down the row until she was close enough to hear the girls. Iona was stuffed into the box Dad's new work boots had come in. Marilyn heard the sad strains of *We Are Going Down the Valley One by One.* Then with great dignity, Twila read Psalm 23 from her old Bible and made some comments. Suzanne led in a prayer much like those prayed in church. Then they sang *Safe In the Arms of Jesus.*

"Now it's time to bury her," Twila said, handing the shovel to Rita. "You first."

Suddenly Michael's burial flashed with sickening reality through Marilyn's mind. *What horrible foolishness to bury that silly old chicken!* she thought. She felt like stopping them.

They finished burying Iona and patted the ground smooth over the top. Suddenly Rita wailed as though her heart were broken.

"Now what's the matter?" Marilyn heard Twila say impatiently. "We did everything like we did for Michael's funeral."

"I know, but I wanted to keep a feather, a beautiful brown feather, and I forgot . . ."

"It's too late now," Twila said firmly.

"Dig her back up," Suzanne commanded. "It'll only take a minute, anything to stop that awful screeching."

Anger swept through Marilyn. She *had* to tell Mother about the wicked funeral the girls were conducting. She dropped her hoe and ran for the house. Mother was folding towels at the dining table. She listened to Marilyn's agonized account of the chicken funeral.

"I knew about the funeral," she said calmly.

"But how could they do such a thing, Mother?" Marilyn wailed. "And so soon after we buried our baby brother! Don't they have any sense of decency at all, Mother? And they sang hymns, Mother. And prayed. I think that's awfully irreverent!"

"It wouldn't be right for you to do it, Marilyn, because you're older and have a better sense of respect for life and death. Children just accept things as they come. It's perfectly normal for them to sometimes play out a funeral, just as they do any other kind of playing. They sang hymns because those are the only songs they know. And Iona did need to be buried. Maybe somehow, this funeral may help Rita accept the deaths of Michael and her pet better than any other way."

"Well, I hope so," Marilyn said grudgingly. "But what was so awful, they dug her back up to get a feather! There are all kinds of feathers in the chicken yard."

Mother smiled sadly. "But none you could be sure was Iona's. I can understand her wanting to keep something. Perhaps I'm just as guilty. Come to the bedroom with me, Marilyn."

On Mother's dresser was a miniature cedar chest. She pulled open a little drawer, took out a small blue envelope, and gave it to Marilyn. Marilyn opened it. Inside was a card on which was taped a wisp of auburn hair.

"Is it Michael's?" Marilyn asked softly.

Mother nodded, her eyes full of tears. "I wanted something real, something I could touch. So I snipped a little hair from the back of his neck. It was longest there. Was I wrong,

Marilyn? Is Rita wrong to want a bit of Iona?"

"No, I guess not," Marilyn admitted slowly. She touched the soft snip of hair, not noticing the tears coursing down her cheeks. After awhile she wiped her eyes and handed the card back to Mother. "Thank you for showing it to me, Mother."

"Be kind to the little girls, Marilyn. Try to see things from their perspective. That'll help, I'm sure."

When Rita came in later with her little brown feather and wondered plaintively how she could keep it safe, Marilyn taped it to a card and put it in a rose-embossed envelope from her own birthday stationery. The little girl threw her arms around her. "Oh, Marilyn," she said happily. "You are the understandingest sister. Thank you! Thank you!"

Marilyn felt a glow of peace and comfort come over her. "I really am sorry you lost your pet, Rita," she said softly. And she meant it.

Before June was over, a truck came and left a cardboard-covered block in front of the garage. The girls knew it was Michael's grave marker. When Dad came home, he broke the metal straps and removed the cardboard. A hush settled over the little group as they read the inscription on the soft-gray stone.

Dad looked up at Mother and the girls. "Are we satisfied?"

"It's just fine," Mother said. "It's exactly what we ordered."

Rita ran her fingers over the engraving and haltingly read the words, then traced the birds, flowers, and lamb. "It's so pretty, Daddy. Do we have to put it in the cemetery?"

"Of course we do," Suzanne interrupted. "It's going to be the prettiest one in Babyland too."

"That's no way to talk," Dad reproved her. "But I am very pleased with it. After supper, Mother, would it suit to take it out and set it on the slab Uncle Jerry and I have ready?"

Mother nodded, and they hurried through supper. The evening was sweet and balmy as they drove the several miles to the cemetery. With solemn respect they watched as Dad carefully set the grave marker in its place among all the other little stones. Already grass covered the earth above Michael's grave.

Dad slipped his arm around Mother. "Well, that's the last thing we can do in memory of Michael," he said softly.

After a moment of silence, Suzanne piped up,

"Now for the picture. Remember we brought the camera, Dad."

Dad took a close-up picture of the grave, and then one of the girls kneeling near the grave marker. For a moment the bitter thought flashed through Marilyn's mind, *A picture of a cold, gray stone is a poor substitute for a live, cuddly baby.* But it was all they had. After she took a picture of Dad and Mother by the marker, they were ready to go home.

Driving out the tree-shaded lane, Twila said thoughtfully, "This cemetery will never seem the same to us again. For now we have a baby buried here. It will be special to us . . . always."

"Except the funny thing is, I don't feel the least little bit like Michael is really here," Suzanne said firmly. "He's in heaven with Jesus. I know he is!"

As she so often did, she had stated the truth for them all.

Chapter 8

Path Through the Woods

It was really too warm to be riding bike. The hot July sun beat down on Marilyn's back as she rode out the lane. The sight of her three sisters under the shady maple snapping beans looked very appealing. But Marilyn had learned to enjoy working for Mrs. Graham, even with her unpredictable moods. Sometimes Mother went instead of Marilyn, or if she was going to be mowing grass or weeding flower beds, one of her sisters might go along. But today she was alone.

As she reached the crossroads to turn east, an old pickup truck roared up from the west. *Oh, no!* muttered Marilyn to herself, *that's the creepy fellow who followed me to Grahams once before.*

In rising panic, Marilyn pedaled faster, but the truck pulled up beside her, its radio blaring loudly. Marilyn wondered how anyone could stand such awful racket. Suddenly the radio switched off, and a voice called, "Hey, girl! You're mighty pretty."

Marilyn was terrified. She braked abruptly and almost lost her balance in the soft dirt along the road. The truck also slowed. When she sped up again, the boy kept pace with her, still yelling out the window. Ahead of her, Marilyn could see the smooth green of the Grahams' lawn. Gasping for breath, she desperately pumped the pedals, then braked and swerved sharply across the road behind the truck, swooping down the ditch and up to the lane.

She leaped from the bike, letting it drop with a crash. Opening the door without calling, she ran into the living room and sagged onto the footstool beside Mrs. Graham.

"Lands, girl!" Mrs. Graham exclaimed with alarm. "Why did you ride so fast in this heat? It's 94 degrees out there. You'll get a heat stroke for sure. Why, you look as if you've been chased by a monster, or worse."

"Maybe I was," Marilyn answered in a trembling voice that didn't sound like her own. Her heart pounding, she told Mrs. Graham what had happened. "But maybe I get scared too easily," she added.

"How absolutely nasty!" Mrs. Graham slammed her fist against the arm of her chair. "You had a right to be scared. I'm sure it was a Nash boy from down on Spur Road, probably Rod. His dad's in jail most of the time, and his mom, Sally, spends most of her time watching soap operas. Her two boys bum the country."

Marilyn shivered and moved closer to Mrs. Graham. "May I work inside today?" she asked.

"Of course. I don't blame you for being unnerved. The idea of that Nash boy terrorizing a girl like you, someone who never did an evil thing in her life. It makes me mad!" She put her large hand tenderly on Marilyn's shoulder. It was the first time she had shown affection for Marilyn. "I'm giving somebody a call!"

Still weak, Marilyn began to clean the bathroom. She could hear Mrs. Graham's angry voice talking to someone on the phone. "And if you don't keep better track of your son, he's going to be parked in the county jail keeping company with his dad," Mrs. Graham said emphatically. Marilyn knew she was talking to Sally Nash. Although Marilyn didn't approve of Mrs. Graham's methods, she did hope she would never get such a scare again.

When it was time to leave, Mrs. Graham said, "I've called your mother to watch for you down your road, and I'm going to get in the wheelchair and watch from the dining room window. I can see at least halfway to the corner. If anyone bothers you, one way or another, I'll have someone there in a jiffy."

Marilyn made the trip home in record time.

Mother was very upset when she heard the story. "And here I thought we lived far enough from the city that we wouldn't have to worry about things like that," she said. "If a girl can't ride her bicycle a mile and a half without being harassed, it's pretty bad."

The discussion at the supper table was about Marilyn's experience.

"I guess we'll just have to make that path through the woods that we talked about before," Suzanne piped up. "Then Marilyn won't have to go out on the road. Doesn't our woods bump into the Grahams' place at the back, Dad?"

"Yes, it does," Dad nodded. "The line fence is just behind Grahams' garage. What path are you talking about?"

"Oh, way back in the spring we girls thought

94

it would be nice to have a path through the woods so we wouldn't get all scratched up. But I guess we forgot about it."

Mother's eyes lit up. "A path through the woods certainly sounds appealing after a hot day like today!" she exclaimed. "And it certainly would be safer . . ."

"'Cepting if there's a bear out there!" Rita said with big eyes.

"No bears," Dad laughed. "Probably not even deer. Maybe some squirrels, rabbits, skunks, or even a fox, but no bears. Tomorrow is Saturday, and making a path in a shady woods certainly sounds more interesting than trimming windows in a steamy, hot house. We'll have to see what we can do."

"First of all we'd need to mark a route," Mother suggested. "The path should follow the smoothest, most interesting way through the woods."

"That means going through the plum thicket," Twila said. "That was just lovely this spring when the wild plums were blooming. It was so romantic."

"And it should *not* go through the blackberry thicket. That's horrible!" Suzanne decided.

"There's a huge pine tree I think the path

should go by," Marilyn added. "And there's a nice rock to sit on and think. I know right where it is."

Mother laughed gaily. It was the first time Marilyn had heard her laugh so freely since Baby Michael died. "You girls do the dishes, and I'll cut some fabric strips out of that bright pink material Annie Betts gave us. We'll use it for marking out a trail yet this evening, if you hurry."

It was amazing how fast the dishes were finished. Then Mother and the four girls trooped out to the woods. Dad had to finish some other business.

The woods were cool after the warm July day. A slight breeze stirred the leaves. Marilyn wondered why they hadn't thought about the path for so long. Mother looked almost young and happy again as she helped the girls plan the route through the woods, tying the bright strips around saplings to mark the way. They made a wide arc that nearly touched the back line fence and then closed the circle near the edge of the garden where they had entered the woods.

It was dusk when they strolled across the yard. Dad met them behind the garage. He smiled as he gave Mother a gentle hug. Marilyn knew he had also noticed the light in Mother's eyes and was glad. "There must be something special about those woods," he said. "Tomorrow we'll take the day off and clear the path. Marilyn will have a safer route to the Grahams, and we'll have a place to stroll when we want to calm our minds."

"Rita won't have a calm mind out there if she doesn't stop thinking about bears," observed Suzanne.

"She'll get over it," Mother assured them. "A nice path will take the scary notions out of her. And it will be good for all of us."

The next day Dad gathered together loppers, chain saw, string trimmer, and two bow saws. Soon they were busy chopping and trimming and sawing. With amusement, Marilyn noticed Mother giving directions and Dad enjoying it. It was amazing how rapidly the path began to thread its way through the woods.

"We must make it wide enough for two people to walk side by side in their Sunday clothes and not get snagged," Mother decided. "And the branches overhead must not whip even the tallest man's head."

At noon Mother sent Marilyn and Twila into the house to make a picnic lunch. The family ate their apples, sandwiches, and chocolate chip cookies, perched on the big rock or the large fallen log nearby.

"I wonder what that ground cover is that looks like baby pine trees," Mother said as they finished eating. "I know about garden plants, but so many of these plants and trees are strange to me."

"Ask Mrs. Graham," Suzanne said. "She's a plant person, isn't she?"

"I know," Marilyn said as an idea popped into her mind. "Monday I'll gather some specimens and ask her to identify them."

"That would be a good idea," Dad approved.

"It would give her something healthy to think about," Mother agreed.

By evening a complete loop laced through the trees. It needed more grooming where the ground was rough or stubs of saplings still poked up, but it was a lovely, mysterious path that beckoned one into its depths.

When it was nearly dark, Rita began to jump at every little rustle in the bushes. Mother laughed. "I believe it's time for our little girls to go into the house." They followed Mother across the yard.

Marilyn stayed behind. As she drifted slowly

along their new path, a strange peace stole into her heart. She lifted her eyes heavenward, up through the leaves of a huge oak tree, into the star-studded sky. "Thank you, God," she breathed. "Thank you for this lovely day in this lovely woods. Thank you that my family can be happy, even after losing our baby."

When it was time to go to Grahams Monday afternoon, Mother was looking doubtfully at a determined Markie standing beside Marilyn. He had come to spend the day while Aunt Bess went shopping. "Are you sure you want to take him along?" Mother asked.

Marilyn shifted the plastic bag with plant specimens to her other arm and grabbed Markie's hand. "But he wants to come along, Mother. He wants to walk with me on our new path. He wants to help me pull weeds in Mrs. Graham's flower beds. That's what she planned for me to do today. You know Markie's good at pulling weeds. He won't even have to go into the house."

Mother sighed. "Well, I just hope it doesn't upset Mrs. Graham. You know she had a baby once who had . . ." Her voice trailed off.

Down's syndrome, Marilyn finished mentally. *Well, what is so bad about that? Markie is a nice boy, whether handicapped or not!*

At Mother's reluctant nod, Marilyn led Markie out beyond the garden and onto the shady path. Wide-eyed with delight, Markie smiled and smiled, even while he clung tightly to Marilyn's hand.

"Lotta, lotta trees," he said. "I like trees. Green, green trees!"

When they came to the line fence, Marilyn held up the bottom strand of barbed wire and helped Markie roll his chubby body underneath. Then she crawled through, relieved she hadn't snagged her dress. It wasn't very dignified, but it was better than being scared speechless on the road.

After Marilyn got Markie started pulling weeds in the rose garden, she took the bag of plant specimens inside to Mrs. Graham. "We've been working on a path through our woods so I won't have to ride on the road," she explained. "And we wondered what these plants are. Do you know?"

Carefully Mrs. Graham lifted each plant out of the bag and laid it on her lap robe. Her hands caressed each leaf. She ran her fingers over each vein. She seemed to have forgotten Marilyn was there.

"Of course, I know. I'll be glad to teach you," she sighed painfully, "but mind you, it hurts. It hurts to know I'll never go out again and find specimens for myself. It's such a thrill to find a plant you didn't know grew in your part of the country. But you can't understand!"

The bitter despair in Mrs. Graham's voice frightened Marilyn. "You don't have to look at the plants," she said quickly. "I'll throw them out. Maybe we can find a plant book somewhere."

"No, no, I'm glad you and your sisters are interested in Mother Nature. That's a whole lot better than messing around with drugs, alcohol, and nicotine like so many young people."

"God," Marilyn blurted. "We're interested in God because He created nature. Not just Mother Nature."

Mrs. Graham smiled briefly. "You've been taught the Creation Story. Very well, believe what you wish. I'm a humanist. I believe man is master of his own universe. Get me that box of labels in the top left-hand drawer of my desk in the study. I'll label these plants for you, while you work outside. This one that looks like a little pine tree is called ground pine."

When Marilyn returned, Markie had pulled

all the weeds that had come up through the mulch beneath the roses. They moved on to the perennial bed in front of the house. Markie could never work without singing. Soon he was giving a rousing rendition of *Rock Of Ages*. Marilyn was so used to Markie singing that she never gave it a thought. All the Hammonds knew Markie had to sing. He didn't always know the words, but he kept perfectly on tune. He sang one hymn after another.

"Marilyn, Marilyn. Come in here," Mrs. Graham ordered through the open window.

"Finish pulling the weeds around that sedum," Marilyn told Markie. "I have to see what Mrs. Graham wants."

"Who was that singing?" Mrs. Graham asked bluntly when Marilyn appeared.

For a moment Marilyn's mind went blank. *Had she, herself, been singing?* "Oh, you mean Markie? My cousin has been helping me. He likes to pull weeds. He was singing."

"Bring him in here," Mrs. Graham demanded.

Marilyn's heart sank. Mrs. Graham looked upset. Maybe Mother was right. She shouldn't have brought Markie to the Grahams.

Obediently, Markie followed Marilyn into the

house. Mrs. Graham stared at the two young people in disbelief. "He . . . he was singing?" she stammered. "Why he was singing the songs my Grandma used to sing. And it was so beautiful. I just had to see who was singing. And he's one of those . . . like our baby . . ." her voice trailed off into silence.

Mrs. Graham's eyes were fixed on Markie, but she appeared to be seeing something else. Marilyn felt a tightness in her throat. She didn't know what to expect.

Markie stood patiently. He seemed to know there was a question about singing. "Sing some more?" he asked hopefully. "I got lotta songs."

Mrs. Graham smiled wanly. "Sometime," she said. "Sometime you can come back and sing for me." She turned to Marilyn. "Do you think my little girl could have been like him had she lived? What else can he do? Could she have pulled weeds? Could she have sung songs? Could she have been a girl with kind eyes like his?"

"Well, we love Markie . . ." Marilyn began honestly.

"And that makes all the difference, I suppose," Mrs. Graham interrupted. She sighed, "And I didn't love my baby, I'll admit. Well, I've learned something today. I guess I've been a slow learner all along. Here are your labeled specimens. Bring me more anytime. I don't know much about people, but I do know plants."

Abruptly she dismissed them, so Markie and Marilyn walked their delightful way home. As they strolled along, Marilyn thought about the afternoon. She marveled at what moved Mrs. Graham to reveal her feelings. First it was a loaf of brown bread, and now it was her handicapped cousin and a bag of plants.

When they reached home, all thoughts of Nancy Graham fled. Twila, Suzanne, and Rita came flying across the yard. "Guess what?" Suzanne squealed breathlessly. "Aunt Julia and Uncle Jerry have twin babies, just born this afternoon."

Marilyn stared. It was too good to be true. "Are you sure? What are they? Are they all right?"

"A boy and a girl. Grandma said they're just fine. And I say it's not really fair. They get one of each, and we don't get any!" Suzanne stated indignantly.

"Don't let Mother hear you say that. She told us we are to rejoice with them that rejoice, just as others wept with us when we wept," Twila calmly quoted Mother.

"Anyway, maybe they'll give us one," Rita said hopefully. "Maybe they'll give us the boy baby."

"No, they won't!" Marilyn said. "Christians don't give away their babies."

"We're just out, that's all," Suzanne said as she tossed her brown braids defiantly. "Other people get the babies, but we don't. When I fussed, Mother said she doubts there'll be any more babies in our family. She said some mothers have lots of babies, and some don't. The doctor told them Michael was a miracle. And he didn't live!"

All the talk that evening was about Janice and Justin. Marilyn tried to think how wonderful it was to have twins in the Hammond family, especially for Uncle Jerry and Aunt Julia who were starting a family when they were older. But somehow talk of babies made her feel keenly again the loss of Michael. She thought she was resigned to God's will, but that night again she wept into her pillow. Would the hurt ever go away entirely? Could she really learn to rejoice with those that rejoiced? Would she love the baby twins?

Chapter 9

Twins and the Trail

Late one afternoon Marilyn, Twila, and Suzanne were washing red beets, and Rita was sitting under the nearby maple watching them. Every now and then they would give her a light spray from the garden hose to make her squeal. It had been an extremely hot August day. None of the girls minded splashing in the water as they washed vegetables for customers.

Then Dad came walking across the lawn. "Look what I found along the road on my way home from work," he said as he placed something in Rita's lap. Her eyes widened as she felt a small, squirmy creature.

"Oh, it's a little kitty," she cried. "Why was it along the road, Daddy?"

"I don't know. It was by a culvert on that

lonely stretch near the Bedford Marsh. I was driving slowly to see if I could spot any blue herons, and I saw this little cat instead. I drove on a ways, but couldn't get it out of my mind, so I went back and picked it up. I'm sure nobody wants it."

"Well, that was a really nice thing to do," Suzanne said admiringly.

"I want it," Rita said. "It must be lost and lonely without its mother."

Dad grinned. "I was sure you would want it. It's going to take some care to keep it alive, but once it gets its tummy full for a few days, that should do it."

"Let's go warm up some milk," Twila said. "That's what a kitty needs."

"And then make her a bed," Suzanne said.

"And then give her a name," Marilyn added with a laugh.

Dad and the girls trooped into the house. Mother patiently held supper until the kitten swallowed a little milk. "After supper you may try using an eyedropper to feed it some more," Mother suggested. "Put her into this little box, wash your hands, and let's eat."

All during supper while everyone else was visiting, Rita was silent. Suddenly she said,

"Patty! Patty! The kitty's name is Patty."

"A funny name for a cat," Suzanne remarked.

"Hush. I don't think cats are particular about names," Dad said dryly.

The cat would be called Patty. Later in the evening when Rita reluctantly put the kitten back into her box, Marilyn thought to herself, *Now if it will just live, all will be well. She mourned for Iona for weeks. We don't need that again. She seems to have gotten Michael's death and Iona's all mixed up.*

For the next several days it was seldom that one would see Rita without the kitten in her arms. Soon it was a black and white ball of fluff.

"That's going to be the prettiest tomcat around," Dad commented one evening.

Rita was stricken. "Tomcat?" she exclaimed. "But this is a girl kitty. Her name is Patty. She has to be a girl kitty."

Dad frowned uncertainly. "But it isn't a female, Rita. I didn't think to tell you. But as I told you before, cats aren't particular about names."

"But I am," Rita wailed. "Now what can I do?"

Marilyn tried not to smile at her little sister's distress. She didn't know why they had all just assumed it was a female cat and needed a girl's name. "Call him Patrick," she said. "That's about the same."

Rita looked doubtful but knelt on the floor. The kitten was playing under an end table across the room. "Here, Patrick. Here, Patrick," she crooned. The kitten bounced across the room and into her arms, curling around her shoulders, and nestling into the crook of her neck. A satisfied smile brightened the little girl's face. "I guess he likes it just as well," she admitted happily.

Dad chuckled. "As I said, cats aren't particular about names."

A few days later, Marilyn commented to her sisters, "Did you notice Rita seems happier since she has a pet again?"

"And I'm happier too," Twila said emphatically. "I was afraid she'd adopt another chicken. I just couldn't face that!"

The twins were three weeks old, and Marilyn's family had been to see them several times. The younger girls were fascinated by the two babies. There were no more comments about the injustice of it. Suzanne had said her piece and then accepted things as they were. Twila and Rita usually took circumstances as they came.

But it bothered Marilyn. With all her heart, she wanted to rejoice with the others over the darling babies, but she could never hold and cuddle them without feeling a little cheated. It made her feel ugly and ashamed.

One evening Mother asked, "Dad, do you mind if Marilyn and I go over and take care of the twins for Julia? Every evening they are so fussy, and nothing she does keeps them quiet for long. Grandma has been going over, but that's really too much for her. Jerry and Julia are both exhausted. Julia says they never get settled before midnight."

Dad looked thoughtful. "Are you sure *you* are ready for that?" he asked quietly.

"I think so," Mother said. "And where there's a need, we ought not think of ourselves."

Soon Mother and Marilyn found themselves at Uncle Jerry's, each in a rocking chair holding a fussy baby. Aunt Julia and Uncle Jerry put Ricky to bed and took a long walk. They returned relaxed and cheerful. "That was so refreshing," said Uncle Jerry. "We really appreciate you giving us a helping hand."

After the babies were fed, Aunt Julia and Uncle Jerry went off to bed, leaving Mother and Marilyn alone with the twins. As Marilyn held

Justin, she looked at his wide blue eyes, round smooth cheeks, and a pink pucker for a mouth. He appeared almost bald, but mostly it was because his hair was very blonde like Aunt Julia's.

Mother was rocking Janice. She was the same size as Justin but had large, dark eyes and a mop of nearly black hair. She looked almost like a little Indian. Marilyn thought it would have been even nicer if the babies looked alike, but being brother and sister, they were not identical twins.

Mother and Marilyn rocked them, changed them, and at 10:00 fed them their bottles, and burped them. Still the babies fussed. But when they sang *Jesus, Saviour, Pilot Me*, as Mother had done for all of her babies, the twins quieted.

Marilyn snuggled her cheek against the soft down of Justin's head. He felt so soft and warm and smelled sweetly of baby lotion. Suddenly an overwhelming desire swept over her. *If Justin could only be my baby brother rather than a cousin*, she thought. Tears came to her eyes, and she felt the old, painful tightness in her throat. *I mustn't cry and hurt Mother. And I mustn't be so selfish,* she told herself fiercely.

But she did cry. Quickly she wiped the tears with a corner of Justin's blanket. She tried to stifle the sobs choking her, but they would come. She couldn't help it. After a while she grew calmer and stole a glance at Mother. Mother was wiping her own eyes on Janice's blanket!

Mother got up and put Janice into her basket. Then she lifted Justin from Marilyn's arms and carefully placed him into his basket. They pushed both beds down the hall closer to their parents' bedroom door.

"Come, Marilyn," Mother said softly. "Let's go sit on the porch swing before we go home."

It was pleasant and peaceful on the old swing. Marilyn remembered many happy times here with her cousins over the years. They sat and swung gently back and forth without speaking.

After a while Mother asked, "Marilyn, are you struggling with feelings that it's unfair that Uncle Jerry and Aunt Julia have twins, and we are left with no baby at all?"

"Oh, Mother, that sounds so awful, so selfish," Marilyn protested.

"Perhaps so, but we're all human, and sometimes ugly, selfish thoughts do come. It's harboring them that's wrong. Sometimes we need to face squarely what's bothering us. That's why I thought it might be good to come over tonight, besides helping Uncle Jerrys out. Did you love little Justin tonight, Marilyn?"

"Oh, I loved him all right; he's so sweet. But it just hurts, that's all."

Mother squeezed Marilyn's hand. "I understand. That's how I felt too. And I also hurt for you. It is all right to mourn our loss, but we must learn to keep the right perspective and not let sorrow color our lives in a negative way."

"Like Nancy Graham does?"

"Exactly," Mother agreed. "And she's miserable because of it. Now we'd better go home before Dad wakes up and starts to wonder what became of us."

Facing things squarely works, Marilyn thought as she got ready for bed. *I surely feel better about the twins than before we went to take care of them.*

Several evenings later Marilyn's family was having a picnic at the edge of the woods, close to where the path went into the woods. Dad had cleared a space for the picnic table. And he promised Mother before the summer was over he would build a fireplace so they wouldn't have to drag their rusty, old grill so far.

Suddenly a man emerged from the path.

Mother gasped. Marilyn recognized Mr. Graham.

"Well, hello, neighbor," Dad said cordially. "Did you smell our supper? There's still a hamburger left. Help yourself."

"No, no. I'm ashamed I've trespassed like this. But I couldn't help myself once I got on this path." He paused, his eyes bright. Marilyn had thought Bob Graham was an ugly, old man, but he stood before them excited as a boy.

"I made that gate in the line fence like we had talked about at Builder's Supply so your wife and girls could get through more easily when they come to see Nancy. I thought I'd just walk down the path a little—and I couldn't stop. It's cleared so nicely, and those signs identifying the trees and the plants . . . Oh, Alex, if Nancy could just see it, I think it would help her a lot! She almost goes crazy penned up in the house. Putting the deck on the house helped some, but it's the woods she loves." He looked as if he would get on his knees and beg.

"Well, that does sound interesting," Dad said. "You can use our woods all you want, but how can we get Nancy out there? The path is still pretty rough. I just haven't had time to do more to it. These girls don't mind skipping over roots and rocks, and dips and hollows, but that won't work well with a wheelchair."

"I've ordered an electric wheelchair for her, and that will help some, but the path will have to be smoother. I have a friend who will let me have all the sand and gravel I want from an old gravel pit on his place. The gravel has clay in it, so most people don't want it, but it would pack nice and smooth. He even has a loader. I'm sure I could have all I want."

"Whoopee!" Suzanne squealed, clasping her hands. "What a bike path that would make! Let him do it, Dad!" she begged.

A look from Dad, and she was quiet, but her eyes were shining with hope.

"Do whatever you like," Dad said to Mr. Graham. "I'll help all I can. You may use our garden tractor and trailer to get back into the woods. I have a lawn roller to pull behind the tractor to make the path smooth and hard."

"I'd sure appreciate it," Bob said with a broad grin. "By bringing the gravel here in my truck and starting from this side, I could keep it a surprise for Nancy. If I come home at four instead of five, I could work on it an hour every day, and she'd never know it."

"And the girls and I will keep it a secret too,"

Mother said, her eyes mirroring everyone's excitement. "I wish I could see her when she goes down that path for the first time!"

"I'd expect you to be there," Mr. Graham said firmly. "She values the friendship of you and the girls very highly. She's never been one for making friends. She'd always rather have had plants and trees, but I think she's found that friends are a lot more comforting than green things when the going gets rough. I always tried to tell her that, but she never believed me."

Mother sometimes went to the Grahams in the afternoons now, rather than Marilyn. Mrs. Graham always seemed embarrassed to have Mother work, but she wanted to visit with her. So Mother went. Hearing about Mrs. Graham's condition, some of the church women occasionally dropped in too. Sometimes she would welcome them heartily; other times she was cool and distant. They never knew what to expect. Marilyn was used to Mrs. Graham's ways, and it didn't bother her as much as it had at first, but the women didn't know what to think. They admired the Hammonds for putting up with her.

Dad, Mother, and the girls walked around the trail with Mr. Graham. They discussed where it needed work to make it suitable for a wheelchair. They admired the wooden gate that swung smoothly on its hinges.

"That'll sure beat crawling under the fence," Suzanne said admiringly. "I've already snagged a hole in my dress and got my hair caught. If you noticed, there was still hair in the barbs where you cut the wire."

"I noticed, but I didn't know if it was yours or a dog's," Mr. Graham teased with a grin.

After a neighborly "good night" at the gate, the Hammonds strolled leisurely back down the trail.

"This woods is such a nice, friendly place," Rita said contentedly.

"And there's not a bear in it!" Suzanne chuckled teasingly.

"I think we should call it *Good Neighbor Woods,*" Twila suggested. "Doesn't that sound romantic?"

"Don't get stuck on words," Marilyn said. "But this path surely has been enjoyable, and now we'll get to share it with Mrs. Graham. Maybe we can put up more nature signs after she tells us what some of the other plants and trees are."

"Sometime we'll have a Hammond gathering and introduce the whole tribe to our woods,"

Dad said enthusiastically.

"There's something healing about a woods," Mother added quietly. "But like Mr. Graham said, people are more important. We need both, and sharing our woods with our friends, neighbors, and family is a wonderful idea."

Several days later Aunt Julia came to get some tomatoes to can. She had left Grandma with the twins, so she didn't stay long. Just before she left she asked Mother, "Did you hear Mrs. Weatherby has been left to care for her two Hispanic grandchildren? Their Mexican mother went back to Mexico hoping to annul her marriage and marry the Mexican man her parents had wanted her to marry before she met Anne Weatherby's son. Anne's son paid no attention to the children, and left them alone so much they were reported to Social Services. As you know, Consuela is Ricky's age, and the baby is only nine months old."

"How can Mrs. Weatherby take care of a nine-month-old child when she can barely walk?" Mother asked.

"Well, she is determined to do it. Sue has been going over once a week to help with her washing. Probably now she will have to go more often. Consuela likes to come over and talk since

I know Spanish, but with twins now, I hardly have time. The whole situation haunts me."

"I want to adopt her, but Mama says me and the twins keep her hopping," Ricky spoke up. "And anyway, Mrs. Weatherby wants her own grandchildren."

"We'll have to see if there's some way to help," Mother said thoughtfully.

The tomatoes were loaded and Aunt Julia left.

"Mother, hadn't we planned to get foster children once?" Twila asked. "Are there many children like Mrs. Weatherby's grandchildren?"

"Too many," Mother said. "And, yes, before we knew Michael was coming, we had been approved as possible foster parents. But then we removed our names."

"Couldn't we get our name back on the list again?" Marilyn asked.

Mother sighed. "Well, Dad and I have talked about it. But foster children often don't stay in one home long, and it would hurt very much to love a child and then have him leave."

"Almost as if he died," Twila nodded. "That would hurt, that's for sure. But, Mother, you said once that it is better to have loved and lost, than to never have loved. Wouldn't that be true about foster children too?"

"I'm sure thinking that way is the only way you could keep foster children, unless you were only doing it for money," Mother admitted.

"There should be some way to get a baby around here, if some folks who have them don't want them," said Suzanne. "Well, I plan to pray about it."

"You do that," Mother said quietly. "But remember to ask for God's will."

Chapter 10

The Tree Hunt

The four Hammond sisters were husking corn at the edge of the garden where they could fling the husks onto the compost pile. "I can't figure it out," Suzanne said in a puzzled voice. "Last spring I was so glad when school was out, I didn't think I'd ever want to go back. And now in just three days we're going to start school again, and I'm so excited!"

Marilyn smiled at her younger sister. "That's how it is every year," she agreed. "I guess we just need a vacation to get us enthused again."

Rita patiently picked up Patrick, her furry little cat, and rearranged him on her shoulder where he often snuggled, hindering her work. "Now I'll get to go to school every day," she said happily. "And I have three new dresses: a blue one, a pink one, and a yellow one. I'll wear the blue the first week, the pink . . ."

"You'll change dresses when Mother tells you," Marilyn interrupted her, "and if you're like Suzanne, that'll be every day."

"She's not like me. Maybe she can stay cleaner. She's more p'tickler," Suzanne admitted cheerfully. "Here comes Mother. She must need more corn to cook up." Mother was blanching the corn and cutting it off the cob for the freezer.

Mother's eyes were twinkling, and she held a notebook in her hand. "I need some help," she said. "Remember I suggested we have a tree hunt when the Hammonds all come over tomorrow evening? I decided it should be like a treasure hunt. We'll have little poems for clues. Listen to this one:

> Stretching lofty to the sky,
> Squirrels love it. I know why.
> Sighing branches, pitchy smell,
> All alone in little dell.
> Are there other trees so fine,
> As this majestic, huge _____ _____?

"White pine!" Twila finished the poem. "Oh, Mother, you are a splendid poet. How did you ever do it?"

Mother laughed. "I guess cutting corn inspired me. Maybe you can help as we finish up the corn. What other trees should we include in the hunt? It will have to be ones we've marked."

"The plum thicket," Suzanne suggested.

"Those twin red oaks just back of the picnic area." Marilyn said. "We should be able to make a poem about them."

"That pretty tree with white skin by Marilyn's thinking rock," Rita said.

"That's a white birch," Twila said. "There are several out there."

"But the sign is close to the one by Marilyn's thinking rock," Rita persisted.

Mother looked amused, but Marilyn was embarrassed. She knew Rita called it her thinking rock because Marilyn liked to sit on the huge, gray, granite rock and think. The younger girls couldn't imagine just thinking, without dolls, books, or cats to entertain themselves. They thought Marilyn was strange and sometimes told her so.

Mother smiled understandingly. "I guess you need a thinking rock just as I needed the cozy crotch in the old box elder tree behind the garage at my girlhood home," she said. "What other trees shall we include?"

"That basswood tree along the south side of the woods," Twila suggested. "It's the only basswood we found."

"The thorn apple tree is interesting and should be easy to find, except nobody better walk under it with bare feet," Suzanne said.

"What about that elm tree that died of Dutch elm disease?" asked Marilyn. "It has lots of holes where one could hide a poem."

Twila's mouth twitched. "Especially since Suzanne collected all that woodpecker dust from them. It's hard to believe, Mother, but she has a whole freezer bag full of woodpecker dust, those shavings woodpeckers make when they're pounding holes!"

"So!" Suzanne defended hotly. "I can collect woodpecker dust if I want to. They don't want it. They've got the bugs all pecked out!"

"I used to collect rocks when I was Suzanne's age," Mother said. "I had a huge box full of them, so heavy I could hardly carry it. After several years I took the whole box outside and filled up a hole in the driveway with them. But I had the fun of collecting them while they interested me. If Suzanne enjoys woodpecker dust, I guess it's harmless enough. Well, that's probably all the trees we'll need for a nice, educational tree hunt."

"Here come's Bob Graham, and Dad's right behind him," Suzanne exclaimed. "Oh, Mother, may Rita and I go help them finish up the trail? This is the last evening, and it'll be done. Please, Mother, the corn's all husked!"

With a nod from Mother, the two younger girls went scampering across the yard toward Mr. Graham with Patrick meowing after them. After Dad greeted Mother and the older girls, he went to help. Marilyn thought longingly of the cool woods and the winding, hard-packed path that Mr. Graham and Dad had worked on so diligently. Sometimes they had all gone to help or to admire the day's progress. Mrs. Graham still knew nothing of their secret. Marilyn wondered when Mr. Graham would at last bring his wife out to see it. She hoped Mrs. Graham would like it.

While they finished bagging the corn, Mother, Marilyn and Twila worked on the tree poems. Maybe their work helped them think, because by supper time most of the clues were finished. "We'll divide the cousins into two groups," Mother decided cheerfully, "and give them each a poem card to get started. They can each begin from a different point so they won't collide with each other, but they'll end up at the same tree. We'll hide a large bag of miniature candy bars in the birch tree by Marilyn's thinking rock, and that will be the prize. Of course, there will be enough to share with the whole group."

Marilyn was glad to see Mother enthused. Since Michael had died, Mother seemed absent-minded and a look of thoughtful sadness sometimes shadowed her face. But lately there was more often a bright liveliness in her gray eyes.

The next day was busy as they got things ready for the picnic supper. All the Hammonds would bring food, but Mother would barbecue chicken on the outdoor grill Dad had built. It had plenty of room to grill chicken and roast corn in its husk. They also made potato salad and whoopie pies.

Mr. Graham and Dad came home early. "Mother," Dad asked. "do you have time to come with the girls and me back through the woods? Mr. Graham is going to bring Mrs. Graham onto the trail. He says he can't wait another day. I know you're busy but . . ."

"Of course, I'll come," Mother said. "I wouldn't miss it for anything."

The Hammonds trooped through the woods.

It had never looked lovelier. Marilyn was so excited her heart was pounding. Mrs. Graham just had to appreciate what they had done. Mr. Graham would be so disappointed if she didn't. But Mrs. Graham was so unpredictable, who could tell how she would respond?

They met Mr. and Mrs. Graham at the gate. Impulsively, Suzanne threw open the gate, and called, "Come into our woods, Mrs. Graham! Hurry, come on in! It's our *Good Neighbor Woods*. We want you to see all our trees and plants and flowers."

Mrs. Graham had a dazed look as the battery-powered wheelchair whispered down the trail. Suddenly she stopped and spread her hands out yearningly as if to gather the whole woods into her arms. "It's so lovely," she cried. "It's been so long since I have heard, and smelled, and felt the soul of a woods."

"Well, it was your husband's idea," Dad grinned. "It's our woods and Bob's work, and it's for your pleasure and ours. All of God's handiwork is here for us to appreciate and thank Him for. I think the girls are hoping you'll help them identify even more plants and trees."

"Oh, I'll be glad to!" Her eyes opened wider as she looked around. "Why, you have already identified some of the trees . . . just like a real nature trail!"

"Say, Mrs. Graham, just around the bend is a tree we can't figure out," Suzanne blurted. "Would you happen to know this one?"

Mrs. Graham's eyes were alight as she inspected the tree Suzanne pointed out. "I'm quite sure it is a blue beech," she said excitedly. "I'll check it with a book I have at home, but I'm quite sure."

"What about this one?" Mother asked a little further down the trail. "We think it's some kind of cherry."

"It's a black cherry," Mrs. Graham agreed. Her cheeks were flushed.

She's almost pretty! Marilyn thought with surprise. It was her sour look that had made her appear unattractive before.

They covered the entire trail, Mrs. Graham often stopping to exclaim about something. She noticed things they had never observed. *She is a teacher, and we could learn a lot from her*, thought Marilyn. *It's too bad summer is nearly over.*

At last they were back at the gate.

"Thank you, thank you, Alex and Mary Ann, for letting us come into your woods," Mrs.

Graham said. "I've certainly enjoyed it."

"You're welcome anytime," Dad said. "And say, we're having a Hammond gathering tonight. Quite a few of my family are coming over, and we're going to eat outside in our new picnic area. Why don't you folks come back over in about an hour and eat with us? We'd be glad to have you."

Mr. Graham looked longingly at Mrs. Graham but said nothing. Mrs. Graham grimaced and looked at the ground, her fingers plucking at her skirt. Finally she looked at Mr. Graham, "Well, I'm not much for people, as you all know. But, Bob, I know you're not much for woods either, and yet you did all this backbreaking work for me. Turnabout is fair play, as the old saying goes." She turned to Dad. "We'll come tonight, Alex. I know Bob wants to. We don't have many friends and relatives, and he misses being with others. I never have, but . . ."

She turned abruptly and began wheeling toward their house on the smooth path Mr. Graham had made for her. With a triumphant wave of his hand, he followed.

By 6:00 a host of Hammonds swarmed over the lawn and back to the picnic area, carrying food, lawn chairs, and blankets. Aunt Julia and Uncle Jerry laid the contented twins in the playpen Mother had set up away from the smoke. Grandma sat nearby in her favorite lawn chair with the peaceful smile she wore when her family was all gathered together.

"Need help?" Sue asked Marilyn, who was grilling the chicken and turning the smoke-blackened ears of corn. Marilyn handed her the tongs and turned to wipe her watering eyes. No matter which way she turned, smoke still came her way. Dad's chimney didn't draw quite right, but it wouldn't seem like a cookout without the smell of smoke and sizzling meat.

Jeff and Steve sauntered over. "Say, that food smells wonderful!" Steve said. "We hurried awfully fast to get the chores done, and I'm famished. I don't think I can wait another minute. You couldn't give a poor beggar something to eat, could you, Marilyn?"

"No, I couldn't," Marilyn laughed, "but if you can just hold out for a few minutes, you can have all you want. There, Dad's calling the children in so we can pray and get started serving."

Just then Mr. and Mrs. Graham came winding into view. Dad welcomed them warmly and introduced them to some of the other Hammonds. Uncle Loren asked the blessing and everyone crowded enthusiastically toward the food. For a time, Marilyn and Sue were kept busy serving chicken and the dangerously hot roasting ears. Then they served themselves and settled on a blanket off to the side where some of the older girls were sitting.

In a remarkably short time, the younger children finished eating and went whooping down the trail. None of them had seen it since it had been groomed and graveled by Mr. Graham and Dad. Marilyn knew that before twilight, all the grown-ups would have leisurely gone the length of the trail too.

When everyone was finished eating, Dad whistled for the children to gather. Everyone seventeen and under was invited to join the tree treasure hunt. He numbered them off by twos and appointed Jeff and Sue captains of their groups. When they understood the instructions, Dad gave out the first cards.

"Go!" Dad shouted, and they were off down the trail. Some of the older ones grabbed their smaller cousins' hands, and away they went.

Marilyn and her sisters stayed behind because they had helped prepare the hunt.

"I not know about trees," Markie said, his bottom lip jutting out. "I stay here."

Mrs. Graham was nearly bouncing in her chair. "I think a tree hunt is a wonderful idea! I can't stay here. Do you mind if I trail those youngsters through the woods? Come, Markie, come along. This is so exciting!" And she wheeled away through the woods, with Markie trotting along behind her.

Marilyn and her sisters ran here and there, caught up in the excitement of their enthusiastic cousins. It was so much fun hearing the jubilant shouts when a group found a clue and were on their way to search for another tree. At last there was a wild clapping, and Marilyn knew a group had found their treasure near her thinking rock. Soon everyone was gathered around the huge rock under the loveliest birch tree in the woods.

"Hey, this was great fun," Barry said, munching a candy bar. "This woods is wonderful. Sometime I'd like to come over and learn what all these trees, bushes, and plants are. Imagine having a nature trail right on your own place!"

"And we've got a neighbor lady who can teach us anything we want to know. Right, Mrs.

Graham?" Suzanne put a friendly hand on Mrs. Graham's shoulder. The older woman beamed. Marilyn marveled at how well those two got along, considering they were both so outspoken.

The candy bars were all eaten when suddenly Ricky stuttered fearfully, "Let's get out of here. It's getting terrible dark. There might be bears!"

Instantly the younger children streamed down the trail. When Jeff saw Ricky's terror, he reached for Ricky's hand. "It's all right," Jeff said, and they jogged toward the fire.

Marilyn gathered up the stray candy wrappers. "Here, I'll hold them," Mrs. Graham offered cheerfully. Marilyn smiled to herself. It was fun making their relatives happy, but even better was sharing a nice time with an embittered neighbor woman.

No Hammond cookout ever ended without singing around the fire. Dad added wood until the golden flames leaped high. First they sang old favorites, such as *How Great Thou Art, What a Friend We Have In Jesus, My Jesus, I Love Thee,* and *Blessed Assurance.*

When the older ones drifted into silence, the young people sang on. Marilyn's throat tightened with emotion as they began to sing:

Some people say there is no God up in
   the heavens,
They say He did not send His Son for us
   to die:
They mock His name and to their shame
   they live without Him.
But I believe in God and I can tell you
   why. [1]

Marilyn wondered what Mr. and Mrs.
Graham were thinking. What did they think of
this Hammond gathering? She knew what she
thought. She was grateful to know her Creator
and to enjoy the closeness of a large family who
shared their convictions with song and prayer
and gentle laughter.

Chapter 11

Shopping With Grandma

At the supper table Suzanne laid down her fork with an important air. "And guess who was in our woods this afternoon?" she asked.

Mother looked startled. "No one besides Nancy Graham, I hope," she said. "When I was over she was planning to go out for a while."

"But she was all by herself," Twila explained. "This is the first time we've seen her by herself. She had a notebook and said she's going to record all the plants and trees she can find. She said our woods is typical of the woods in Lincoln County. By studying our woods, she will learn about what she would if she went into a lot of other woods."

"And she said something funny," Suzanne added. "She said someone said if the world hands you a lemon, you should make lemonade. She said she's going to make lemonade. Now whatever did she mean by that? When I asked her, she said I should ask you, Mother. She said you've been making lemonade all summer."

Suzanne looked so puzzled that Marilyn had to smile. Suzanne went on, "But, Mother, you didn't buy lemons even once this summer."

Dad chuckled. "I think I can explain. Lemons are terribly sour, and you can hardly stand to eat them unless you cut them up, put them in a pitcher of water, and add sugar. Then they make a refreshing drink. Troubles can be sour and disappointing like lemons. But if you make the best of even bad circumstances, then they can be a blessing. Mother lost her baby, which made her very sad. But instead of becoming bitter, she's been helping others. That is what Mrs. Graham meant."

"Well, that makes sense," Suzanne said. "I guess if she can't go everywhere she wants, she can at least look around in our woods."

"You ought to see her notebook," Twila said. "She draws pictures of what she sees. She draws lots better than I can. We asked her a bunch of questions."

Suzanne giggled, "And then she got kind of

grouchy and told us we ask more questions than a Philadelphia lawyer, so we went and played on the other side of the woods."

"You must not irritate Mrs. Graham," Mother said. "I'm happy she's trying to get out and do something profitable. I do wish she could learn what the Bible says, ". . . that all things work together for good to them that love God."

"She ought to go to church," Rita said solemnly.

"Once I asked her to come to church with us," Suzanne said. "She said it would be a hot day in January before she goes to church. I guess she meant she just won't go, because we never have hot days in January. Mrs. Graham says funny things."

"Not very funny," Dad said. "But whether Mrs. Graham ever goes to church or becomes a Christian has nothing to do with whether we are good, kind neighbors, or not. We should be loving no matter what Mr. and Mrs. Graham do. That's what God expects."

After washing the dishes, the Hammonds went out to rake leaves. The October evening was balmy and pleasant, and the family enjoyed working together. By the time they had dragged the last tarp full of leaves to the compost pile, a glowing harvest moon was hanging in the sky.

"You know what?" Rita said wearily as they walked toward the house. "We don't have our baby, but we can still be a happy family. Tonight was fun."

"Be more fun with a baby," Suzanne said stoutly. "I'm still praying."

A few days later, Mother hung up the telephone and turned to Marilyn and Twila just coming in the door. "That was Grandma Hammond. You girls have no school on Friday because of a teacher's meeting. Grandma was wondering if you two would like to go along to Greenville with her. Sue is taking her for a doctor's appointment. Grandma thought it would be nice to take her granddaughters along since Uncle Jerrys can't go this time."

Twila's dark eyes sparkled. "Oh, that would be great fun! May we go, Mother?"

"I can't see why not. Perhaps Grandma would take you to the big fabric store in Greenville. You've both grown so much you could each use another school dress."

"You mean we could choose our own material?" Twila asked in surprise.

"With Grandma's approval, of course. And

before you leave, I'll give you a price range and the amount of material you would need," Mother said. "It will be a good experience for you."

Early Friday morning, Sue and Grandma Hammond drove in the lane. After Mother gave Marilyn and Twila money and last-minute instructions, they ran to the car.

"Good morning, girls," Grandma greeted them warmly. "I consider this a real privilege to have three granddaughters along."

"Do you trust my driving?" Sue asked with a merry smile. "We won't be going downtown, because the stores we like are near the clinic at the edge of Greenville. I don't feel comfortable in heavy traffic."

"If the driver's license examiner said you're a safe driver, I'll believe him," laughed Marilyn.

An hour later they were parking at the clinic in Greenville. Marilyn and Twila waited in the waiting room, while Grandma and Sue went in to see the doctor. Grandma wanted Sue along because Grandma was a little deaf and didn't always understand the doctor's orders. Marilyn and Twila watched the other people in the waiting room. They were so interesting, it didn't seem long at all until Grandma and Sue were back.

Next they went to the fabric store. Like most girls, Sue, Marilyn, and Twila were fascinated by the array of dress material.

"Mother said we should get printed polyester-cotton fabric," Marilyn reminded Twila. "She said that would be best for school dresses. This table probably has something." They looked carefully. Marilyn found a medium blue with tiny pink flowers she thought was pretty. She went to see if Twila had found anything.

"Do you like this?" Twila asked, her hand resting on a grass-green fabric dotted with a gay assortment of large, bright flowers.

Marilyn couldn't believe her eyes. "Do . . . do you?" she stammered.

Twila's eyes sparkled. "Yes, I do. It reminds me of that field next to the church with beautiful wildflowers all summer long. I've never seen fabric like this before."

"Neither have I," Marilyn said honestly. She didn't know what else to tell Twila without hurting her feelings.

"Do you think Mother will like it?" Twila asked anxiously.

Marilyn was quite sure that Mother wouldn't like it at all. It was too bright and gaudy and would look horrible on Twila. But Marilyn knew that to Twila's eyes, the fabric was beautiful.

To Marilyn's relief Grandma came up just then. "And have you decided on your material?" she asked.

Marilyn held out the bolt of blue cloth and Grandma's eyes brightened. "That's nice," she agreed. "I always like blue."

"Do you like green?" Twila asked. She held up the material for Grandma to see.

An uncomfortable look came into Grandma's kind eyes. "Well, that's plenty green, my dear, too green. Especially with those big, bright flowers. I think your Mother would prefer something more modest. Let's see if we can find something else."

Twila looked bewildered. Marilyn felt sorry for her. Twila meekly followed Grandma. They agreed a light green fabric with dainty pink and yellow flowers would be a better choice.

After Grandma bought a wedding gift at Price-Mart, they went to The Burger House for lunch.

When they were nearly finished eating, Twila said hesitantly, "Grandma, you didn't think the green material was modest. How can material not be modest? Don't you just buy plenty so the dress is long enough and not tight anywhere when you're done?"

Grandma's face was thoughtful. "Modesty is more than just covering your body with plenty of material. It also means wearing clothes that don't draw extra attention to yourself. The green fabric was so eye-catching and colorful that you would have stood out anywhere you went. I don't think you really want that."

"Grass and flowers are bright, and God made them. Why shouldn't we be bright too?" Twila asked wistfully.

"I think it is because God gets glory from the color and shape of flowers. But people glorify Him from beautiful, Christ-like souls, not fancy clothes," Grandma said seriously.

"I'd almost rather be a flower," Twila sighed.

"That might seem nice, but remember, flowers can't love or be loved like people, and in the end they wither and die too." Grandma crumpled up her napkin and gathered up her jacket and purse. "I think you girls are beautiful just as God made you," she added with a smile.

Marilyn liked Grandma's explanation of modesty, and was sure even Twila would understand with time.

At a secondhand shop, Grandma bought some

old-fashioned overshoes she needed for winter. The girl's found many things they wanted, but nothing they really needed, so they came out empty-handed.

The grocery store was their last stop, and then they headed for home. Sue drove, Grandma sat wearily with her eyes closed, and in the backseat Marilyn hummed to herself. Twila read billboards along the highway.

"Adoption, Not Abortion," Twila read. "What does that mean, Marilyn? I know what adoption is, but what is abortion?"

Marilyn sighed. "Grandma, you explain to her. You're good at explaining."

Grandma turned to look at Twila. "Well, I suppose you should know," she said. "We live in a wicked world, Twila. Sometimes a mother finds out she's going to have a baby, and she doesn't want it. She has a doctor kill the baby before it is ever born. That is murder. It is wicked. Many people don't want to believe an unborn baby is even a real person. The sign is saying if you won't love and care for your baby, at least let it be born for someone to adopt."

A look of horror darkened Twila's eyes. "You mean there are people who don't *want* their babies, who want to get rid of their baby? And here we wanted our baby so bad, and we couldn't keep him. I think this world is all mixed up!"

"It is, Twila," Grandma agreed. "We need to accept death as God wills, but we must never accept murder. It's very disturbing to think about. You may want to talk to your mother more about it."

Twila settled into her corner, a troubled little figure. Marilyn noticed she read no more billboards.

When they arrived home, the two younger girls came bouncing out of the house, eager to see what they had bought. They were delighted with the fabric.

"You'll look great in green," Suzanne said to Twila. "Maybe you didn't buy enough, and I can have it."

"I bought plenty," Twila said with a satisfied air. Marilyn knew the gaudy material they left behind would be soon forgotten.

"We got to do something special today too," Rita said, shifting Patrick to her other arm where he drooped like a furry, black-and-white purse. "We went to Aunt Julia's to help can pumpkins. Uncle Jerry took Ricky with him, so Suzanne and I played *all day* with the twins. They are the dearest little things. We each got one, and they didn't fuss a bit."

"I liked Janice best today," Suzanne said. "I told Aunt Julia I'd like to keep her, even if she is a girl. But Aunt Julia said she wouldn't give her up for all the world."

"I should think not!" Twila flashed vehemently. "Some people do perfectly horrible things to their babies now-a-days, but Aunt Julia wouldn't!"

Suzanne was startled at the heated words from usually mild-mannered Twila. But for once she didn't ask for an explanation.

The four sisters trooped into the house. Mother was hurrying to fix supper before Dad came home. "Did you have a nice time?" she asked, smiling.

"We surely did," Twila said. "It was a *very* good experience."

Twilight was falling as the happy family gathered around the supper table. "Our Heavenly Father, we thank Thee . . ." Dad began to pray.

Chapter 12

Robbie

"Oh, look at me!" Rita squealed. She was lying on the ground, swooping her arms and legs back and forth making angels in the snow.

"You're going to be wet and cold before we get to the house as many angels as you have made," Marilyn reminded her.

Rita got up carefully and studied her imprint in the snow. "It's the best one yet," she said happily.

"She can't resist any new patch of smooth snow," Suzanne said in a grown-up way. "I used to be like that too."

The girls were on the path through the woods. They had stopped with Mother to visit Mrs. Graham after school. The girls had begged to tromp home through the woods while Mother went by the road. A fresh snowfall had made the woods a winter wonderland.

Marilyn brushed the snow off her thinking rock and sat down on the cold surface. *Where has winter gone?* she thought to herself. *It's hard to believe this is already the middle of January, not even a year since Michael died. And everyone seems so content. How can it be? That must be what folks meant when they said time heals. And yet sometimes I wonder if the hurt can ever really go away . . .*

"Ohoooow!" Marilyn shrieked, her thoughts forgotten, as a shower of powdery snow fell upon her. The girls giggled. Twila's dancing eyes told Marilyn who was guilty.

"Wake up, Dreamy Eyes, or you're going to freeze to that rock," Twila said.

"How can you just sit there when it's so beautiful out here?" Suzanne asked. "I thought it was lovely this summer, but look at it now! Everything's so white and blue-ish. The trees are dark, and the brown ferns stick through the snow and, well, it's too bad Mrs. Graham can't come out and see it."

"I'm cold," Rita said with a whimper, "and it's starting to get dark. Let's go home."

Marilyn jumped stiffly off the ice cold rock,

grabbed her youngest sister's hand, and the girls threaded their way through the snowy woods toward the welcome lights of home.

After supper the family gathered in the living room for devotions. They were reading in 2 Samuel. Dad began by reviewing what they had read the evening before. "So David realized he had committed a great sin against the Lord in taking Bathsheba for his wife and killing Uriah, her husband. Now let's take turns reading the rest of Chapter 12. Marilyn, you begin."

An odd feeling gripped Marilyn as they began reading. She knew how the chapter would end and her heartbeat quickened. At verse 23 it was Suzanne's turn. Suzanne's reading was often halting, but this verse had simple words, and she read through it easily.

"I know, Daddy, I remember." Suzanne lifted her brown head excitedly. "These are the words Brother Don said, 'I shall go to him, but he shall not return to me.' Remember? We can go to Michael . . ."

Mother took a sharp breath and put her hand to her cheek. Marilyn knew what Mother was thinking. The memory still hurt.

Her own throat felt tight as she remembered

the day of the funeral—the last look at Michael's little face, the small coffin lowered into the ground, the dark patch of dirt scarring the green earth, and now the smooth gray stone engraved with birds and a lamb that simply said, *Michael Alex Hammond.*

Twila got up and gave Mother a tissue. Dad's voice was unsteady as he finished reading the chapter. Then he prayed, "Our Father, we thank you for your comfort and your promises. We believe You do all things well." His deep, sincere voice prayed on, and Marilyn was comforted.

That night in bed, Marilyn thought about sorrow. *Why, after all this time, does it still hurt? Maybe it's like an injury. You think it's all healed until you accidentally bump it. And then suddenly it will hurt terribly for a little while. But each time it is less. But I wonder, does sorrow ever completely heal?*

Several days later, Mother dropped Markie and Marilyn off at the Grahams after school. Markie was staying with the Hammonds while Aunt Bess and Uncle Loren were on a trip. When Markie had found out that Marilyn was going to help Mrs. Graham, he had stated firmly, "I go along. I work. I sing."

He had gone with the girls a few times before, but it had been a while. Marilyn sighed. You never knew what to expect from Markie, or from Mrs. Graham either for that matter.

Mrs. Graham met them at the kitchen door. Sometimes she used a walker to get around in the kitchen. It always startled Marilyn. Mrs. Graham was a big woman and towered over Marilyn, making her feel small and insignificant.

"Hello," she said abruptly. "So there are two of you today. You feeling ambitious? I want these cupboards cleaned out. Bob spilled a box of corn flakes and made a mess, and . . ."

"I help," Markie said. "And I sing."

"You will, will you?" Mrs. Graham said. She sighed, "Well, I could use some singing. I'm sick and tired of this house. I'm sick and tired of being penned up. I'm tired of messing with specimens when I can't get any more. If you come here and find me stark, raving mad, you'll know it's because I can't stand being handicapped—diabetic, one-legged, and useless."

"I help, and I sing," Markie repeated.

"OK, then," Mrs. Graham said irritably. "I'll quit griping, and you can work. There's a little brush in the broom closet to sweep up that cereal. I'll be in the living room."

Marilyn started Markie cleaning out the silverware drawer while she cleaned up the messy cereal shelf. When she finished, she went on to other shelves. As usual, Markie began singing and Marilyn joined in. They sang all the old favorites, Markie singing soprano and Marilyn alto. Sometimes they made mistakes and laughed together.

When they finished the cupboards, they went into the living room.

"So you've finished," Mrs. Graham said. "I enjoyed the inspirational service." She was silent for a moment. Marilyn wasn't sure if she was serious or sarcastic.

Mrs. Graham sighed and went on, "Sometimes when I hear Markie sing it's hard to be a humanist. A humanist believes a person must be a contribution to society to be a part of it. According to that, Markie should never have been born. And me, what am I contributing to society? Markie, with his singing, is using his talents better than I!"

Markie looked confused, and Marilyn was uncomfortable. What could she say?

Mrs. Graham stirred restlessly in her chair. "If there is a God, I'm sure He is a God of justice.

I guess it's justice I am handicapped, considering I didn't want my handicapped baby."

She sounded so remorseful that Marilyn leaned forward eagerly. "But, Mrs. Graham, God is also a God of mercy. He'll forgive you, if you ask Him to."

"*Come, ye sinners, poor and needy* . . . Yes, I heard you singing that. My grandmother used to sing it too. But I'm not ready to reckon with that notion of sin."

Mrs. Graham sighed. "Well, I heard your father drive in. You two had better go. Thank you for your singing and work. I have something to think about, whether I want to or not."

Friday evening Mother picked the girls up at school. "Aunt Julia called today," Mother said. "She said Mrs. Weatherby had a bad fall on her porch steps this afternoon and has broken her hip. She is in the Greenville hospital."

"That's too bad," Twila mourned. "I like Mrs. Weatherby, especially since she's been coming to church and we've gotten to know her. She's so grandmother-ish."

"What about Robbie and Consuela?" Marilyn asked. "She was taking care of them by herself except when Sue went over to help with the washing. Was Sue there when it happened, Mother?"

"No, she wasn't. She was there yesterday but not today. No one was with Mrs. Weatherby. A neighbor found her lying outside and called the ambulance. She was cold and in agony."

"Are the children home alone?" Rita asked in horror.

"No, the ambulance crew notified the sheriff's department about the children. Social Services went and got them," Mother replied.

"Social Services!" Suzanne exclaimed. "Aren't they the folks who give out foster children?"

"Yes, they're to see children are cared for when their parents aren't able to, or won't," Mother agreed.

Suzanne gave an excited bounce on the front seat. "Well, I thought the Lord would figure something out so we could get a baby! I think He's going to give us Robbie, if Mrs. Weatherby can't take care of him."

Mother glanced at Suzanne. "Suzanne," she asked sharply, "you haven't been praying something bad would happen to Mrs. Weatherby so she couldn't keep Robbie, have you?"

Suzanne was indignant. "I really want us to

have a baby, but I'm not mean enough to wish a broken hip on Mrs. Weatherby. She's kind, but you know she's plenty old to be keeping a baby anyway."

When they got home, the girls couldn't keep Mrs. Weatherby's accident out of their conversation.

"I'm glad Mother and Dad put our home back on the list for a foster baby," Suzanne declared. "I'm just positive we'll get Robbie."

"Maybe Mrs. Weatherby's son will come back for his children," Twila suggested. "Or the children's mother."

"Their father is in the military in Germany, and their mother is remarried in Mexico," Marilyn said. "I don't think it's very likely they'll want the children. Sue said Mrs. Weatherby never hears from either one. But even if we get Robbie, what will happen to Consuela? The folks only put their names in for preschool children, and Consuela is in second grade."

"Well, if we can just get Robbie, I'll be satisfied," Suzanne said.

"How do you think Mother feels about it?" Twila asked Marilyn. "Where is she anyway?"

"Mother's vacuuming the baby's room," Rita

announced, coming in from the back hall.

The girls looked at each other excitedly and smiled.

At 7:30 the telephone rang, and Mother answered. The girls saw her face grow pale . . . then pink. "Oh, yes! Yes, certainly. Of course!" She carried the cordless phone out to the garage where Dad was working.

"I knew it," Suzanne exulted. "They want us to keep Robbie."

"How come you think you know so much?" Twila snapped. Her face was tense. Marilyn had a sudden ache inside as she thought how disappointed they would all be if they couldn't keep Robbie.

When Dad and Mother came in from the garage, they were smiling. Dad said, "Do you want a little brother for awhile? Social Services says Robbie needs a home for an indefinite period of time, and we're the ones chosen for the responsibility. What do you say, girls?"

"Wonderful! Marvelous!" shouted Suzanne. "It's about time."

"When will he come?" asked Marilyn.

"Tomorrow morning," Dad answered.

"What about Consuela?" Rita wanted to know.

"We made a mistake there," Dad said regretfully. "We never thought about brother-sister situations, and Consuela is going to another home. I don't know whose. It's too bad they need to be separated."

"I only hope she gets into a good home," Mother said.

"I guess that means more praying," Suzanne said matter-of-factly.

The girls were so excited, they could hardly settle down to sleep that night. Marilyn imagined Dad and Mother were having the same trouble because she heard the murmur of their voices far into the night.

When a blue car pulled into their driveway the next morning, the whole family was assembled in the living room. "Girls," Marilyn said tensely, "he doesn't know us, so we'd better not frighten him by all wanting to hold him at once."

"I'll be satisfied just to look at him," Suzanne retorted. "But don't think you get him the most just 'cause you're the oldest!"

A neatly dressed lady came to the door carrying Robbie, warmly dressed in a green snowsuit. Dad invited her in. She took off Robbie's snowsuit and set him on her lap where he could see the family.

"He's fifteen months old and gets into every

thing," said Mrs. Gunther. "So please make sure all cleaning products are under lock and key or completely out of reach. Stairways will need to be gated. I see your electrical receptacles are already covered. Carefully read all the guidelines we gave you to refresh your minds. With your girls you have plenty of help to watch out for him, but babies his age need a lot of watching. If you have any questions call the number in the folder I will leave with you."

Mother asked questions about Robbie's health, his teeth, immunizations, and sleeping habits. All the while Robbie gazed at them with big, brown eyes. His skin was a creamy color, lighter than Consuela's, and his hair was almost black.

The lady laughed as she looked at Dad. "He could almost be your son, your coloring is so much alike."

Suddenly Robbie reached out his arms for Marilyn and whimpered. "S-S-S-S!"

"I believe he thinks you're Sue," Mother said. "She's been over there often."

Mrs. Gunther handed Robbie to Marilyn who reached for him eagerly. She could hardly believe she was the first to hold him. Mother looked pleased.

"At least he wants to come to us," Mother said.

The girls crowded around Marilyn and Robbie while Mother and Dad covered final details with Mrs. Gunther about Robbie's stay. Dad went out to her car and brought in a large box with Robbie's clothes. In another moment, Mrs. Gunther was gone, leaving little Robbie in the Hammond family's care.

It was a glorious Saturday. Very little cleaning got done. The girls would no more than begin sweeping a floor, dusting a bookcase, or cleaning a sink, and they would drop their broom, dust cloth, or cleaning rag and run to the living room to see what Robbie was doing. They waited for turns to hold him. Dad came into the house every so often to see how they were getting along.

Robbie was a friendly baby and enjoyed all the attention. Finally Mother suggested they put him down so he could explore on his own. It did not take long to understand what Mrs. Gunther meant about him getting into everything.

"I guess we haven't had a toddler in the house for so long, I forgot what it was like," Mother said happily. "We'll put some things up, and the rest he'll just have to learn to leave alone."

They put his clothes in the drawers, his diapers in the diaper stacker, and got out all the baby products that had been put away. Baby toys Mother had kept in a back closet were gotten out and put into a basket on the floor. All the bedding for the crib was washed and dried.

In the afternoon Mother rocked Robbie in the rocking chair until he finally fell asleep. She tucked him into the crib. There he slept like a little angel.

"Finally we have a baby in that crib!" Suzanne whispered exultantly.

"It looks just right," Rita glowed with satisfaction.

"I hadn't liked this room much for a long time," Twila said softly. "But now I think it'll be the nicest room in the house."

Mother laughed as she partly closed the door. "You'll think that until sometime when he's howling at the top of his lungs. He will do his share of fussing. He's a very normal little boy, and we're glad for that. But I know what you're talking about," she added soberly. "In this room before, we thought of death. But now we'll think of life!"

All the rest of the day the family marveled. There was finally a little boy in the family. You could see it on every face. There was laughter and song and an excitement flowing through them all. Marilyn noticed a light in Mother's eyes that hadn't been there for a long time. When Dad swooped Robbie up and tucked him into the high chair at supper time, it put a lump in Marilyn's throat. She remembered how he used to do that to Rita to make her squeal.

But in the back of their minds, they also knew Robbie's stay was not a permanent arrangement.

That evening before going to bed, Twila was combing out her long, dark hair in front of the mirror. Suddenly she turned to Marilyn. "How does that saying go Mother told us once about Michael. 'It's better to love . . .'?"

" 'Tis better to have loved and lost than never to have loved at all,' " Marilyn quoted.

" 'Tis better to have loved and lost than never to have loved at all,' " Twila repeated. "We're going to have to remember that, Marilyn. But I really believe it, don't you?"

Marilyn stood for a moment, thoughtfully plumping up her pillow. "Yes, I do, Twila. Since losing Michael, we know it's true. Yes, I do."

"Then I plan on loving Robbie all I want," Twila decided.

Marilyn smiled at her sister as she reached for her Bible. "So will I," she said firmly.

Chapter 13

In Memory of Michael

One afternoon Marilyn sat at the dining room table carefully pinning the hem on a new dress spread in front of her. A merry squeal made her glance up at the spring world outside the window. "Oh, Mother!" she exclaimed. "Can you see how Robbie is enjoying his wagon ride? The girls are pulling him up and down the sidewalk as fast as they can, and he's hanging on for dear life!"

Mother chuckled from where she was working at the kitchen sink. "He certainly has been enjoying these warm days. As soon as you girls come home from school, all he can say is 'bye-bye!' and that means he wants *out!* Twila said they pulled him all around the woods trail."

"Isn't it muddy out there?" Marilyn asked.

"It was a couple days ago. But it had just rained."

"Mr. Graham went over the trail with the lawn roller yesterday, and the sun has been shining all day," said Mother. "Twila said it's smooth and dry. They met Mrs. Graham with a bag full of specimens in her wheelchair. After we said she could dig plants, Mr. Graham designed some kind of folding hoe she can dig with. Twila said she seemed especially cheerful. Mrs. Graham made a big fuss over Robbie. The girls thought it was really unusual. They've heard her say some awful things about babies."

"I have too," Marilyn said, trying to thread a needle. "But Mrs. Graham is changing in a lot of ways. I don't mind working for her anymore."

"We've had some good talks when I visit," Mother said. "She is doing a lot of thinking. She is an intelligent woman, but very set in her ways, and her ways are the ways of many worldly women."

Happy laughter from outside made Marilyn sigh wistfully. "I'm just aching to be outside, Mother. But I want to finish this dress for the spring school program, and that's only a week away. The other girls have theirs about all finished."

"Well," Mother teased, "the garbage needs to be dumped, and the chickens would be glad to see it."

At last the children's joyful shouts drove Marilyn to fold her dress and take it to the sewing room.

Mother smiled as she handed Marilyn the garbage pail. "Tell Suzanne and Twila to come in," she said. "If Robbie's still warm enough, you can stay out with him until supper time. Dad should be home within a half hour."

Marilyn delivered her message and carefully set the garbage pail behind Robbie so he wouldn't get his grabby little hands into it. Then she pulled him to the chicken house.

"Chickie, Chickie, Chickie," Robbie trebled as the chickens cackled and squabbled over the garbage.

"He can talk pretty well," Rita remarked, as she watched Robbie in the wagon. As usual Patrick was draped around her neck. He was getting to be a pretty hefty cat. "Robbie can talk almost as well as Markie."

"What he says is pretty clear," Marilyn agreed. "But he doesn't know very many words."

"Enough to tell us what he wants," Rita said. "Grandma Weatherby will be excited to hear him talk when she comes over for dinner Sunday. Mother invited her. Grandma Weatherby's leg is well enough now that she can come to church and to our place."

"Do you think she wants you to call her Grandma?" Marilyn asked doubtfully.

"Of course. She says she needs all the grand-children she can get, 'specially since Consuela is so far away."

"Out. Sandbox. T'uck," Robbie said insistently.

Marilyn laughed. "We sure know what you want, Robbie!" She lifted him from the wagon and cuddled his grubby little body against hers. He gave her a generous hug and a sloppy kiss, then struggled to get down. Once on the ground, he scampered for the sandbox and was soon playing happily in the moist sand.

Marilyn and Rita sat in the glider swing, the late afternoon sun shining warmly in their faces. Both Rita and Patrick looked sleepy, snuggled together in their corner. Marilyn watched busy little Robbie and thought deep thoughts.

It's almost a year since Michael was born and died. A year ago we were eagerly looking forward

*to his birth, and now all we can remember is his
death. Strangely, there are days when we're so
busy, I don't think about it at all. I wonder if
Mother ever forgets to think about Michael. I
should ask her sometime. Since Robbie came it's
easier to forget. Is that wrong? We'll never forget Michael. Never! But Robbie is so sweet.
Somehow he makes the hurt less. It's too bad
about Consuela. We hardly ever see her. I wish
she could be our sister too.*

A small hand on her knee brought her out of
her reverie. "M'lyn! Daddy! Come!"

"So Daddy came home, did he?" Marilyn
laughed. "Let's go find him." She scooped him
up, and the three headed for the garage where
Dad was unloading his truck.

In a moment a little boy was getting a bear
hug from a beaming father.

That evening Mr. Graham came over and
talked with Dad in the garage for a long time.
Dad came in looking sober. After the girls were
in bed, Marilyn heard Dad and Mother's muf-
fled voices. She didn't know what they were dis-
cussing, but she was sure it had something to
do with Bob and Nancy Graham.

That Saturday was Michael Alex Hammond's
birthday. In the afternoon Mother and Dad went

to town. When they returned, Mother said, "The grass is green over Michael's grave, girls. We must soon plant some flowers by the marker. Be thinking about what you would like." Her eyes looked tired, and she said nothing more.

After school Monday, Dad came to pick them up. "I'm surprised to see you, Dad," Twila said. "Didn't you go to work today?"

"Were you working in the garden?" Suzanne asked.

"Is something special going to happen?" Rita asked.

Dad grinned. "Such questions. And just because a father comes to pick up his daughters! But, yes, Mr. Graham has something special in mind. As soon as we get home, they're coming over."

"They?" Suzanne questioned again. "How is Mrs. Graham coming over, through the woods?"

"Not this time," was all Dad would say.

When they arrived home, a shiny blue van was parked in their drive. Mr. Graham, Mrs. Graham in her wheelchair, and Mother with Robbie, were waiting in the sunshine in front of the garage.

Mr. Graham seemed as eager as a small boy. "See, girls," he said. "I bought a van to take

Nancy around in. It has a wheelchair lift, so we can go anywhere, even on trips if we want to. Come, I'll show you how it works."

He wheeled Mrs. Graham to a platform resting on the ground. After fastening the chair in place, he pressed a button, and the platform rose slowly to the level of the van floor. Then Mr. Graham pushed her inside. "I certainly hope that lift doesn't give out when I'm halfway up," Mrs. Graham sputtered, but her cheeks were flushed and her eyes bright. She looked almost as excited as Mr. Graham.

"That's great," Dad said sincerely. "Now you won't feel so housebound. You can do your own shopping or whatever you want. I've seen many folks in wheelchairs about town."

For a moment a shadow passed over Nancy's face. "But I never thought I'd be one of them," she said.

"It could be any one of us," Dad said. "You today. Me tomorrow. Who knows. But we can make the best of things, and it looks like this van could really help you out."

Mrs. Graham smiled briefly. "In other words, make lemonade. Okay, Alex, I understand."

"Let's go," Mr. Graham said. "I had them put the bench seat in back, and there's room for one of you girls up front with me. Your mother and dad and the baby will be coming in your van. We have some things to see this afternoon."

Where can Mr. Graham be taking us? Marilyn wondered. *It has to be something Dad has approved.*

It did not take them long to find out. Bob drove directly to the cemetery, but not to Babyland. In the opposite corner, he guided Mrs. Graham and the Hammonds to a small grave marker.

Nanette Graham
B. July 8, 1973; D. Oct. 21, 1973
In The Arms of Jesus

"I just put it in last week," Mr. Graham said quietly. "I saw how nice your baby's marker looked. It didn't seem right that our baby's grave should have been so long without a marker." His voice became anxious. "Do you like it, Nancy?"

Her words faltered. "Yes . . . yes, Bob, it looks nice. But . . . do you really think . . . do you think she's with Jesus?"

Marilyn felt almost as if they shouldn't be there, the moment seemed so sacred. Mr. Graham looked into her eyes. "Yes, Nancy, I do.

And somehow, I'm going to find out how to make sure that when my time comes, I'll go there too. There's something to this Jesus story, Nancy. I believe it."

"Our baby with Jesus?" Mrs. Graham repeated, belief and doubt struggling within her. Tears filled her eyes, and suddenly she was sobbing, her head bowed in her hands. Marilyn could hardly believe it.

"There, there, Nancy," Mr. Graham said awkwardly. "I didn't mean to make you cry. I didn't think you'd mind now. I wanted to share this day with our friends. Just a year ago they buried their baby. I knew they'd understand. Don't cry, Nancy."

"Let me cry," Mrs. Graham sobbed. "I've never cried before. Not ever. Let me cry now."

Mother and the girls could not help weeping with the distraught mother.

After a time Mrs. Graham quieted. "My poor little baby," she said sadly. "I could have loved her. You folks love Markie. But she died, and I didn't care. I've been a hard woman, Bob. I've wept seventeen years too late for my own baby. I can't quite believe the baby is with Jesus. But you believe it, Bob. Keep believing it. I want you to."

They moved down the graveled path to Babyland and gathered around Michael's marker. Rita bent and traced her finger over the letters spelling out her only brother's name.

Dad and Mr. Graham talked about Michael's birth and death. Mother and Mrs. Graham listened sadly.

"Well, I guess we should go, Bob," Dad said. "This is your day. You lead the way." Marilyn wondered where they were going next.

As they started towards the vans, Twila said wistfully, "You know, when we come here, I always think it will make me feel closer to Michael. But it doesn't. Why?"

Suzanne stopped and stared at her. "Because he's not here, Twila. You know that! Probably nothing of him is here but a bit of dust. He's with Jesus! You can't feel close to somebody who isn't here."

Mrs. Graham looked at Suzanne with amazement. "Such faith," Marilyn heard her mutter to her husband. Trust Suzanne to say something exactly as it was!

They got into the vans, and Mr. Graham led the way to the other end of town. "The nursery is on the right side of the street," Mrs. Graham said.

Rita stared at her, her eyes enormous. "Are you getting a baby?" she asked.

Mrs. Graham laughed. "A baby tree, perhaps. This nursery sells plants and trees. We've discussed it with your parents. We are going to plant trees in each of our yards in memory of our babies. Bob and I are going to pay for them."

"Oh, goody," Rita said. "Looking for a tree will be fun."

One section of the nursery was a forest of small trees growing in pots or burlap.

"I know what kind of tree I want," Mrs. Graham said. "I want a weeping willow tree to plant in the corner of the yard where it's low and damp most of the time. A willow will grow well there."

"What kind of tree do you want, Mother?" Marilyn asked.

"Perhaps a flowering tree," Mother said thoughtfully.

The girls wandered in and out among the trees, reading the tags with names and prices. Suddenly Suzanne whooped, "Here, I found one. It's blooming! It looks like an apple tree."

"It's a Radiant crab apple," Twila read the label. "Mother, would you like a crab apple tree?"

Mother's face brightened. "Yes, I would. They are beautiful. But that's an awfully large tree. It'll probably be too expensive."

"If you like it, we'll take it," Mr. Graham declared.

The nursery man came. "This tree is blooming a little too early because it's here in the sun near the pavement. I'd rather sell you a tree that's not blooming yet. Come with me, and I'll find you one even nicer."

The younger girls were disappointed, but Marilyn knew the tree they carefully placed in Mr. Graham's van was nearly perfect. The man promised it would have some blossoms in a few weeks. The Grahams' willow was already leafing out and looked like it would become a beautiful tree. With a satisfied feeling, they left the nursery parking lot.

Mr. Graham drove directly to the Grahams. There he and Dad dug a large hole while the girls unreeled the long garden hose until it reached right to the tree. After planting the tree, they watered it.

"I can see it right from the living room window," Nancy said with a pleased smile. "I'm just sure I can. It will be wonderful to watch it grow."

Mr. Graham put the crab apple in the garden cart because it wouldn't fit in the Hammond van. "You folks just drive around to your place, Alex, and we'll come on the trail. You girls want to come with us?"

"Let me hold Robbie? He likes the woods, I know he does," Mrs. Graham insisted. "He can ride on my lap."

Mother looked a little doubtful.

"Wide! Wide!" Robbie said, and soon he was perched on Mrs. Graham lap, thrilled with this unusual ride.

"Isn't this amazing?" Twila whispered to Marilyn, as they filed down the woodland path.

"This whole afternoon has been amazing," Marilyn murmured back.

The crab apple tree was planted in the front lawn where it could easily be seen from the living room window. Mother's cheeks were flushed with pleasure. "I can just see it a fragrant mass of pink in a few years," she said. "Thank you, Bob and Nancy, for this wonderful idea."

Mrs. Graham smiled. "You're welcome, Mary Ann. It's a small price for your friendship, I'm sure. And now we'd better be getting home. None of us has had supper yet, and this child is falling asleep without it."

"Wait a bit, " Mother said. She ran into the house and returned with a jar of home-canned vegetable soup and a loaf of fresh bread. "For your supper," she said. "We'll have the same."

After supper Twila disappeared. Sometime later she came to Marilyn in their bedroom. "Please, come with me, Marilyn," she begged. "Come out to the garage."

Two small signs with black letters painted on a white background lay drying on the workbench. "They're not really neat," she said apologetically. "I'm not so good with letters. But I wanted to do it." Her dark eyes begged for approval.

For a moment Marilyn wished she would have thought of it. She could have lettered the signs more neatly. Then she said sincerely, "It's a wonderful idea, Twila. I know where Dad has some stakes. That paint looks dry. We'll nail the signs to the stakes and put ours up tonight. We can take the other one over to Grahams tomorrow. They'll be delighted."

The girls got busy, and soon the sign and stake were nailed together. Marilyn found the sledge hammer. A little way from the trunk of the new crab apple, she pounded in the stake.

"There, how does that look?" she asked.

175

"Good!" Twila said. "Now shall we show the others?"

Twilight was falling, and the mosquitoes were beginning to buzz as the family gathered around the little tree.

"In Memory of Michael Alex Hammond," Dad read softly.

Silence settled over the little group. Robbie gave a sleepy whimper and stirred. "Let's get this little fellow to bed," Dad said gently. They walked to the house, a peaceful and contented family.

It really is true, Marilyn thought, *God does work all things out for good.*

Christian Light Publications, Inc., is a nonprofit conservative Mennonite publishing company providing Christ-centered, Biblical literature in a variety of forms including Gospel tracts, books, Sunday school materials, summer Bible school materials, and a full curriculum for Christian day schools and homeschools.

For more information at no obligation or for spiritual help, please write to us at:

Christian Light Publications, Inc.
P. O. Box 1212
Harrisonburg, VA 22801-1212